# The Little Vampire in Love

'Don't you want to hear the latest about
Rudolph?' asked Anna . . . .
'What did you say?' Tony asked absently.
'I want to tell you something about Rudolph.
You'll never guess – he's fallen in love!'
'In love? Who with?'
'With the Honourable Olga Pigsbubble. But
you're not even listening to me!'

Tony is rather nervous of Anna now she has
grown her fangs, but the vampire children
are still his best friends. So when the Little
Vampire falls for Aunt Dorothy's dreadful
niece, Olga, Tony knows he must help
Anna sort her brother out. But helping
vampires – especially vampires in love – is a
blood-curdling business!

This is the fifth book about the Little
Vampire. The others are:
*The Little Vampire, The Little Vampire Moves
In, The Little Vampire Takes a Trip, and The
Little Vampire on the Farm.*

# Little Vampire

## The Little Vampire In Love

**ANGELA SOMMER-BODENBURG**

Translated by Sarah Gibson

Illustrated by Amelia Glienke

**Hippo Books**
**Scholastic Children's Books**
**London**

Scholastic Children's Books,
Scholastic Publications Ltd,
7-9 Pratt Street, London NW1 0AE, UK

Scholastic Inc.,
730 Broadway, New York, NY 10003, USA

Scholastic Canada Ltd,
123 Newkirk Road, Richmond Hill,
Ontario, Canada L4C 3G5

Ashton Scholastic Pty Ltd,
P O Box 579, Gosford, New South Wales,
Australia

Ashton Scholastic Ltd,
Private Bag 1, Penrose, Auckland,
New Zealand

First published in West Germany by
Rowohlt Taschenbuch Verlag, 1985

First published in the UK by Andersen Press Ltd, 1986

Published in paperback by Scholastic Publications Ltd, 1988

This translation copyright © Andersen Press Ltd, 1986
Original title Der kleine Vampir und die grosse Liebe

ISBN 0 590 70792 2

Made and printed by Cox & Wyman Ltd,
Reading, Berks.

Typeset in Palatino by J&L Composition Ltd, Filey,
North Yorkshire

10 9 8 7 6 5 4 3 2

This book is for Burghardt Bodenburg, who has finally got his vampire teeth (from the dentist), for Katja and for everyone who still believes in true love – as I do.

Angela Sommer–Bodenburg

# Contents

# 1

# 'She'

Tony came back from the pottery class tired and hungry. He opened the front door of the flat and sniffed appreciatively at the smell of roast potatoes which greeted him. He quickly hung his jacket in the cupboard and went into the kitchen.

His father was sitting at the table cutting a cucumber into thin slices. 'Hello there, Tony,' he said, and added with a mysterious smile, 'you've got a visitor!'

'Me? A visitor?'

'Yes. She's waiting in your room.'

'She?' repeated Tony in bewilderment. 'In my room?'

His father grinned. 'You've gone quite red!'

'I have not!' retorted Tony. He was sure that 'she' could hear every word they said!

In a whisper, he asked: 'Who is it?'

His father laughed and would not say. Tony stomped furiously out of the kitchen.

A girl — visiting him at home — at half past seven in the evening ... he did not know whether to be pleased or annoyed! Cautiously he opened the door to his room — and saw Anna sitting on the bed.

She had switched on the lamp and was reading, her head bent over a book. Her brown hair was carefully brushed and you might have thought she was a perfectly normal girl — except for the faint smell of decay and her torn black vampire cloak!

Tony stepped into the room, took a deep breath and said, 'Good evening, Anna!'

She looked up from her book. When she saw Tony, her pale cheeks coloured pink.

'Tony! At last we're together again!'

She put the book aside and came up to him smiling. Tony gazed transfixed at her mouth: her eye teeth had grown long and pointed! She noticed his look and blushed. 'There's no need to be frightened,' she said. 'I'd never do anything to you.'

Tony's head buzzed and he did not know what to say.

'Aren't you pleased?' she asked.

'Pleased? Pleased about what?'

'That I've become a proper vampire! Now Rudolph can't call me "Anna the Toothless" any more, "the only member of the family who lives on milk"! I'm now known as "Anna the Fearless"!' She drew herself up and laughed. 'But you still look as though someone's thrown a bucket of cold water over you!' she exclaimed, puzzled.

'I . . . ' murmured Tony, who had retreated to the door. 'It's just that I've got to get used to your, er, vampire teeth.'

'Yes, so have I,' she agreed. 'Suddenly everything is so different. Except you — I like you just as much as I always have.'

Tony realised he was going red. He quickly turned away and looked at the window. It was closed. 'How did you get in?' he asked, relieved to be talking about a less awkward subject.

'Through the door. I came up in the lift and rang the front doorbell.'

'Weren't you scared of my parents?'

'Yes, I was. But then I said to myself: Human girls can go to a friend's house and ring the bell, so I must do it too, if I'm to be known as "Anna the Fearless".'

'And? What did my parents say?'

'I didn't see your mother. But your father grinned and asked me if I was off to another fancy dress party. Yes, I said, we're having a party at the sports club tonight.' She rubbed her hands and giggled.

At that moment, there was a knock at the door, and Tony's father came in. 'Well, you two?' he said, and winked at Tony. 'Are you getting along?'

'Yes,' growled Tony, annoyed by his father's conspiratorial tone of voice. 'We were — till you came along!'

'I've got to go now,' said Anna, plucking at her cloak.

'Go?' exclaimed Tony's father. 'But it's almost suppertime. I've put out some cheese especially for you, and a glass of milk — that is what you like, isn't it?'

Tony felt hot and cold shivers run down his spine. But Anna remained calm. 'Thank you so much,' she said. 'That's very kind of you. But I really can't eat with you. There will be hot dogs and chips at the sports club

3

later.' With that, she held out her hand to Tony's father, said, 'Goodbye, I hope we meet again soon,' and left.

Tony went with her as far as the lift.

'Will we see each other tomorrow?' she asked with an eager smile.

'I, er, don't know,' he stuttered.

'Tomorrow's Saturday,' she said. 'Don't your parents always go out on a Saturday?'

He nodded hesitantly. 'Yes.'

'So we two could do something together,' she suggested. 'After all, we have got something to celebrate.'

The lift arrived and she got in.

'Celebrate? Celebrate what?' asked Tony.

'That I'm not "Anna the Toothless" any more,' she answered, and before Tony had time to reply, she closed the door behind her.

## 2

# Clay Figures that I Made Myself

When Tony came back into the kitchen, his parents were already sitting at table and had begun their supper.

'Well, you really missed something,' Tony's father was saying.

Tony's mother looked up. 'Oh? What was that?'

'Tony had a visitor.'

'A visitor?'

'Yes. If you hadn't been in your room buried in your marking, you might have seen Tony's girlfriend!'

'Tony's girlfriend?' she repeated in surprise. 'I didn't know he had a girlfriend.'

'I haven't!' said Tony furiously.

Tony's father was visibly enjoying his embarrassment.

'You should have heard the two of them. They were cooing like turtle doves!'

'Ha, ha, ha,' was all Tony could say. He did not find his father's remarks at all funny.

'And who is this girl?' asked his mother.

'Anna,' answered Dad. 'The one with the vampire cloak.' He laughed, as if at a well-tried joke, but Tony's mother remained serious.

'Anna? That ghostly pale girl who came

5

here once with her brother? The one with the knobbly fingers and dark shadows under her eyes?'

'But that's all part of the vampire costume,' said Dad evenly.

'Exactly,' said Tony quickly. 'And what's more — I can't stand it when you two stick your noses in my business!'

'In *your* business?' retorted Mum coolly. 'I think we have a small say in our own son's friendships. Especially if it's a question of that strange pair with their revolting cloaks. They are certainly not the types for you to be mixing with!'

'Oh? And why not?'

'Because they only encourage your obsession with vampires.'

'Obsession with vampires?' said Tony crossly.

'Yes. There are vampires wherever you look in your room, pictures of vampires on the walls, books about vampires in the bookcase, and if you had the chance, you'd watch videos about vampires from dawn till dusk!'

Tony had to smile in spite of himself. 'So what?'

'Can't we talk about something else?' asked Dad. 'Tell us what it was like at the pottery class?'

'The pottery class? What should it have been like?'

'Didn't you bring any work home with you?'

'Yes — '

'Well? Aren't you going to show us?'

'I don't know — '

'What do you mean?'

'I don't think Mum will like what I've made,' said Tony, stifling a smile.

'Why shouldn't I like it?' replied his mother. 'I like everything you've made yourself.'

'Oh really?' said Tony. He fetched two clay figures out of his jacket and stood them on the table, next to the plate of cucumber slices.

His mother let out a shriek. 'Vampires!'

'Yes, vampires!' said Tony, regarding the two figures proudly. They wore black cloaks and had chalky white faces. Between their lips, which Tony had painted a luminous red, sharp vampire teeth pointed out.

His mother groaned gently. 'And I thought you'd make something sensible.'

'What do you mean? These have turned out brill. Our art teacher gave me an "A" for them.'

'And I was so looking forward to having a vase. . . .'

'Tch . . . ' said Tony. He glanced at his father, and added with a spiteful grin: 'What would you do with a vase? After all, no one ever gives you any flowers!'

Whistling happily, he went to his room.

# Romeo and Juliet

Tony's parents set out shortly after six the following evening. They wanted to see *Romeo and Juliet* and had not yet bought their tickets for the play.

Tony stood in the hall with them as they put on their coats. 'Aren't you a bit old for it?' he asked.

'Too old? For what?' said Dad.

'Well, I mean . . . Romeo and Juliet were a very young pair of lovers, after all — '

His father laughed. 'Oh, so you think love is only for young people, do you?'

'In any case, we want to see the play, not take part in it,' retorted Mum, going to the door. 'Goodnight.'

Dad followed her. 'Sleep tight, Romeo!' he said, and shut the door. Tony nearly choked. Just as well Dad did not know how right he was. Since Anna's visit, he did feel rather like Romeo! He went back to his room and switched on the television.

A couple dressed in pink were singing: 'Only you, you, you and me. . . .' How stupid! thought Tony. But time did go by more quickly if you were watching television.

When the knocking came on his window, Tony jumped up so quickly that he nearly fell over. Anna was sitting outside. 'Hello!' she said. 'Are you by yourself?'

'Yes.' Tony cleared his throat. 'Come on in.'

'Thank you,' she smiled, and hopped down from the window-sill.

'Where is the man, the man for me ...' warbled a woman's voice from the television.

'Music!' said Anna, entranced. She went up close to the screen. 'Do you know who she is?'

'Who?'

'The singer.'

'No.'

'Just look at the beautiful dress she's wearing. It's so white ... just like a fresh fall of snow.'

'I think it's a bit too flash.'

'Too flash? But it must have cost the earth!'

'Exactly.'

'I thought you thought she was pretty.'

'I think you are much, much prettier,' said Tony — and blushed right up to his ears.

Anna's eyes gleamed. 'Really?'

'Yes,' he said in embarrassment, and switched off the television. 'Let's go.'

'Let's fly!' corrected Anna, holding out a second cloak she had hidden under her own. 'Here you are — it's for you,' she said. 'From Uncle Theodore's coffin.'

With a shudder, Tony recognised the smelly, musty old vampire cloak which he had often worn before. It used to belong to Uncle Theodore — before McRookery the

10

Nightwatchman had hammered a stake through his heart.

Uneasily, Tony put it over his head. Then he spread out his arms and moved them evenly up and down. He began to hover.

'Come on!' said Anna, and swooped out into the night.

Still rather unsteadily, Tony followed her.

# 4

# News

The moon was shining brightly and the air was clear and fresh. Suddenly Tony felt free as air and without thinking, gave a little cry of pleasure.

'Can you feel it too?' asked Anna excitedly.

'What?' said Tony.

'This atmosphere — as if the moon had cast a spell over everything. The church tower over there — it could almost be the tower of a castle. And the trees in front of it look like guards.'

'Yes. And that great big one over there looks like a knight on horseback.'

'No, it looks more like Aunt Dorothy!' giggled Anna.

Tony started. 'Aunt Dorothy? Where?'

'Nowhere,' Anna reassured him. 'It was just that that great round tree reminded me of her. But in fact, even that's not true any more: Aunt Dorothy's got much slimmer, now she has to share everything — with Olga.'

'Who's Olga?'

'Her niece. But I'll tell you about her later — once we're in the vault.'

'In the vault?' Tony began to feel peculiar. 'I thought you said we were going to do something together.'

'We are. I just want to give you something first — a present.'

'A present?' Tony wasn't at all sure he wanted a present.

'It's in my coffin,' explained Anna.

'Couldn't you have brought it with you?'

She giggled. 'I wanted you to come and get it.'

Tony did not exactly find the idea of going into the vault with Anna and possibly meeting one of her bloodthirsty relations enticing!

'What about the — the other vampires?' he asked anxiously.

'They're out.'

'What about Aunt Dorothy? And Olga?'

'They're out too.'

He hoped she was right. Up till now, every time he had visited the vault, something unexpected had happened. Once Aunt Dorothy had very nearly caught him. . . .

'I — er, I'd rather wait outside,' he said.

'Outside? That's far more dangerous,' answered Anna. 'McRookery patrols the cemetery almost every night now, with his new assistant gardener.'

'He's got a gardener?'

Anna nodded grimly. 'Sniveller. From Watford.'

'Oh no! Since when?'

'Three weeks ago exactly. I saw a great removals van draw up outside McRookery's house and I watched them taking Sniveller's things inside. The next day, a signboard went up by the door which said: Mr

13

Sniveller, Assistant Gardener. And what's more Sniveller stinks of garlic as well, *and* he carries sharpened wooden stakes around in his pockets. Just like McRookery.' She paused. 'But one night they will have to deal with me!' she said fiercely and shook her tiny fists. 'After all, I am Anna the Fearless.'

'What will you do?' asked Tony.

'I'll think of something,' she said, but her voice sounded rather subdued.

'I'd gladly help you,' said Tony.

'Really? Oh Tony, I could kiss you!'

'I — I'd rather you didn't,' stammered Tony. 'Otherwise we'll fall. Anyway, there's the cemetery wall just in front of us.'

Anna's face took on a tense expression. 'We must be careful,' she said and took Tony's hand. They slowed their flight and landed in the tall grass behind the cemetery wall.

# 5

# The Present

It was the farthest corner of the cemetery. Here, there were no carefully tended graves, no tidily trimmed hedges, no raked paths — only crosses askew and head-stones over-turned. It was all wild and neglected.

Very uneasily, Tony looked over towards the tall yew tree under which lay the entrance to the vault. He hoped Anna was right: that all the vampires really were not at home!

'I promise there isn't anyone in the vault,' he heard Anna say.

He jumped, startled. 'Can you read a person's thoughts?'

She laughed gently. 'No. But I could tell what you were thinking about from the expression on your face.'

'But supposing Aunt Dorothy is lying unconscious in her coffin again?' he objected, in the hope of dissuading her from her plan to fetch the present.

'No. She'll be giving Olga lessons in the park. But I'll tell you all about it in the vault.'

'What about McRookery? And Sniveller?' Tony tried once more to put her off.

'They're over on the other side of the cemetery. I can hear their footsteps on the gravel path.'

'And Rudolph? Where's he?' It was a last attempt to stop Anna going into the vault.

'Rudolph! Rudolph! I suppose I just don't count!' she cried.

'Of course you do,' he soothed her.

'If you must know, Rudolph's got someone else now!' she told him coldly.

'What — what do you mean?'

'You'll soon find out. Let's go.'

Without waiting for Tony's reply, she ran over to the yew tree and pushed aside the stone which covered the entrance to the vault. Then she disappeared.

Tony followed with wobbly knees. But it was better to go with Anna into the vault than to stay out in the cemetery all alone and possibly fall into the clutches of McRookery and Sniveller! They would certainly mistake him for a vampire — after all, he was wearing Uncle Theodore's cloak.

He let himself slide carefully down the narrow shaft and landed in a little alcove: the anteroom to the vault. He quickly pulled the stone back over the opening and started down the steps which led to the vault.

A feeble glimmer of light came from the vault and it smelt of dankness and decay.

'Anna?' he called.

'Yes!' He heard her voice. 'There's no one here — just us two.'

Tony gave a sigh of relief and went forward slowly. The smell of decay grew stronger with every step.

At last he saw Anna. She was sitting on

her coffin and had lit one of the candles in the wall. She looked at him expectantly. Her lips were slightly parted — but only a little way, and her pointed eye-teeth were hidden. She gestured to the space next to her.

'Come and sit here,' she invited him.

'C-coming,' Tony stuttered. He preferred not to be so close to her. 'I'll just have a quick look around the vault first. It all looks so different,' he added.

It certainly did: one coffin now stood quite alone in one corner. It was — the Little Vampire's!

'Why isn't Rudolph's coffin with the others?' he asked. 'Has he made a fuss about something?'

'Yes,' Anna told him with a giggle. 'And if you come and sit next to me, I'll tell you all about it!'

But Tony preferred to remain standing. He pointed to a strange wooden structure which was leaning against the wall. 'What's that?'

'A folding coffin.'

'A folding coffin?' He eyed the black object curiously. It reminded him of his grandmother's folding screen. 'Who does that amazing thing belong to?'

'Olga,' she replied in a grave voice.

'May I open it?' asked Tony, fingering the rusty old hinges.

'No!' said Anna vehemently.

'But I'm interested in how it works!'

'And you're not interested in me at all!' she cried crossly. 'Ever since you've been here, you haven't mentioned the present even once!'

He quickly took the hint. 'Oh yes, the present. What is it?'

She jumped off the coffin and opened the lid.

'There it is — for you!'

Reluctantly, Tony came over to the coffin and looked inside. On the frayed red pillow he spied a small package wrapped in silver paper.

Anna watched him, breathless with excitement.

As he hesitated, she cried impatiently: 'Aren't you going to open it?'

'Of course — ' With shaking fingers he unwrapped it and discovered — a dummy! Anna's dummy! He stared in horror at the well-chewed ancient object!

'Aren't you pleased?' exclaimed Anna.

'Y-yes!' he stammered.

'Here, let me tie it on for you,' she said eagerly and took the dummy.

'No!' shrieked Tony, taking a step backwards.

Anna looked at him with huge, unbelieving eyes.

'Don't you like it?'

'I — er — it's just that I don't need one,' he stuttered.

'Does that mean you don't want it?' she asked, her voice trembling. 'I give you the

18

only thing I possess — and then you don't want it!'

Tony broke out in goose pimples. If he did not manage to pacify Anna, he would really be in the soup! But what should he do? Take the dummy? His stomach turned at the mere thought of it! So he stood there dumb and helpless and watched as she put the dummy back in her coffin and closed the lid.

Then she said frostily: 'Come on, we must fly.'

'Where to?' he asked anxiously.

'To your home,' she answered brusquely and blew out the candle. Tony had to feel his way behind her in the dark to the opening.

She did not say one word during the whole flight home.

'Goodnight, Anna,' he said when they reached his window.

But she merely bit her lips and sailed away in silence.

# A Corpse Come to Visit Us!

For breakfast the next morning, there were home-made muffins. Normally Tony could eat four or five of them, but this time he had lost his appetite completely. Listlessly he spread butter onto a muffin.

'You look very overtired,' remarked his mother.

'So?' was all Tony said.

'Yes. You've got huge shadows under your eyes.'

'Just like a corpse come to visit us!' said Tony's father, and laughed so loudly that he almost spilled his coffee.

'It's because of school,' growled Tony.

'School?' repeated his mother scornfully. 'It's from watching television!'

'If that's what you like to think . . . ' said Tony. He poured himself some milk, stirred some chocolate powder into it and took a mouthful — but even sweet hot chocolate did not taste nice this morning.

'Well, you don't exactly look like a blooming Romeo today!' teased Dad.

'You and your stupid Romeo!' growled Tony.

His father grinned broadly. 'You'd have liked the play, I'm sure. The last Act takes place in . . . a vault!'

'In a v-vault?' Tony was so surprised that he dropped his muffin. 'In a cemetery?'

'Yes. With coffins and shrouds and corpses and people pretending to be dead. . . .'

'Do you have to tell Tony all this?' said Mum disapprovingly.

'Why not?' asked Dad. 'After all, *Romeo and Juliet* is one of the greatest love tragedies of world literature.'

'What's a tragedy?' Tony wanted to know.

'A play with a sad ending.'

'So they don't end up together?'

'Who?'

'Romeo and Juliet.'

'No,' answered his father. 'In the end, Juliet, who has fallen into a deathlike sleep, is buried in the family vault. Romeo thinks she really is dead, so he swallows poison by her coffin and dies. When Juliet wakes up, she finds her Romeo dead — and stabs herself with his dagger.'

'Coo — that must have been quite grisly!' said Tony. 'Were you frightened?'

'Frightened?' Dad laughed. 'A bit.'

'It would have made my heart beat a little,' admitted Tony enthusiastically. 'A cemetery, a vault, coffins, dead bodies. . . .'

'Now just look what you've started,' scolded Tony's mother. 'Now he's off again on his favourite subject.'

Tony raised his eyebrows and looked dignified.

'Dad was only trying to help my education on a bit — after all, you must know what's what on the subject of world literature!'

22

'Oh, I've had enough!' exclaimed Mum, and stood up. She shut the kitchen door behind her with a bang.

Tony looked at his father and grinned. 'Will you lend me the book?'

'Which book?'

'The one about Romeo and Juliet?'

'I don't know if it's quite suitable for you — '

'Of course it is! It all happens in a vault!'

# Time Will Tell

But Tony soon realised his father was right: he could hardly understand a word. He laid the book aside with a sigh and took *Carmilla, the Female Vampire* down from the shelf — a vampire story by Sheridan le Fanu. After all, that was world literature too!

Eagerly, he turned to the first chapter: 'A Sinister Omen'. By the time it was dark outside, he had read the whole book — interrupted by lunch and by saying good-bye to his parents who wanted to go for a long walk — something that did not appeal to Tony in the least.

The strange thing was that earlier, before he knew Anna and Rudolph, he had liked the story much better. Perhaps it was because of the gruesome ending: Carmilla got a sharp stake through her heart. . . . No, Rudolph and Anna must never come to such a sticky end!

His mind turned once more to the vault and to Anna's disappointed face. Should he have taken the dummy and pretended that he liked it? But he could not pretend, at any rate not about that revolting present. Anna was bound to be angry with him still. . . .

A knock at the window roused him from his thoughts. He saw a dark figure peering into the room . . . Rudolph? Happily, he ran over to the window and opened it. On the window-sill sat Anna.

'You?' said Tony in confusion. 'I thought. . . .'

' . . . I was cross with you, didn't you?' she asked. 'But I'm not — not any more. May I come in?'

'O-of course,' stuttered Tony. 'My parents have gone for a walk.'

'What about you?' she said once she was in the room. 'Are you still cross with me?'

'No — ' murmured Tony.

'Of course I was very disappointed that you didn't want my dummy,' she explained, sitting down on Tony's bed. 'But then I thought about it and realised that you don't need a dummy at all at the moment and that was why you weren't pleased with the present.'

Tony blanched. 'What do you mean — not at the moment?'

She smiled and Tony saw her sharp white teeth glisten.

'Simple,' she said gently. 'Because you aren't a vampire yet. It's only when you're a growing vampire that you need a dummy so that your eye-teeth grow long and pointed and your front teeth stay small.'

'But my eye-teeth won't grow any more!' cried Tony.

'Won't they?' she said in surprise. 'Aren't they milk teeth?'

'No!'

25

'I see — so a dummy is totally unnecessary . . . your eye-teeth will grow long and pointed on their own when you become a vampire.'

'But I don't want to become a vampire!' exclaimed Tony.

Anna laughed slyly. 'Who knows?'

Tony would have liked to have contradicted her as strongly as he could — but he did not want to argue with her any more and so simply said, 'I'm quite sure I don't.'

Even so, Anna gave him a loaded look. 'Time will tell,' she said, adding, 'Bide your time and have a cup of blood, er, tea!'

Once more Tony caught sight of her vampire teeth, and a cold shudder ran down his spine.

'I — I've got some homework to do,' he said hastily. Going over to the desk, he began to rummage around in his school things.

'Don't you want to hear the latest about Rudolph?' asked Anna.

Tony gave no answer. He had just decided to write an essay on the subject: What I would like to be when I grow up.

'What did you say?' he asked absently.

'I want to tell you something about Rudolph. You'll never guess — he's fallen in love!'

'In love? Who with?'

'With the Honourable Olga Pigsbubble. But you're not even listening to me!'

Anna jumped up from the bed and came

over to Tony. She read the title in his
English exercise book in an undertone.

'It's such a stupid subject,' grumbled
Tony. 'As if I already knew what I want to
be!'

'Is it homework?' inquired Anna.

He nodded. 'Unfortunately.'

But Anna appeared to have a different
view of homework. 'May I do it for you?
Please?'

'What do you mean?'

'I'll write the essay for you. If I try hard,
no one will notice.'

'But I've got to give it in the day after
tomorrow.'

'No problem. I'll bring the book back tomorrow.' And already she had stuffed the book under her cloak.

'W-wait!' said Tony. Everything was happening rather too fast! 'What are you going to write with?'

'Your pen!' Anna replied, taking Tony's pen which also vanished under her cloak. 'Now shall I tell you about the love of Rudolph's life?'

'The love of Rudolph's life?' repeated Tony in astonishment.

'You see! You just weren't listening at all!' she exclaimed reproachfully. 'I told you ten minutes ago that Rudolph had fallen in love with the Honourable Olga Pigsbubble!'

'In love?' Perhaps this was the reason why the Little Vampire had not visited him for the past couple of weeks. 'Is Olga living with you at the moment?'

'Yes — worst luck. Aunt Dorothy is her only — er — living relative. Olga's parents were killed by vampire hunters in their castle in Transylvania where the Pigsbubble family had lived for centuries.' She said these last words in a voice so full of hate that it made Tony shiver.

'Transylvania? Where Count Dracula lives?' he asked with a hidden shudder.

'In the next door castle,' said Anna darkly.

Tony sighed, partly out of awe for the famous Transylvanian count, partly out of sympathy with Olga. 'How did she manage to travel so far?'

'Her father had a craze on collecting coffins. The most unusual piece in his collection was the folding coffin. She strapped it on her back and flew off with it.'

'But that must have been really exhausting!'

'Yes. But that's still no reason to behave like she does,' said Anna grimly.

'Why? What does she do?'

'She thinks she's superior because she used to live in a castle. There she had servants who had to do everything for her — apparently even find her food for her. Olga can't even catch a rabbit — at least, she acts as if she can't. She relies on us to look after her. Especially on Aunt Dorothy, because she's Olga's aunt. Aunt Dorothy's now trying to teach Olga to hunt and attack, but she hasn't had much luck so far. Olga is just too comfortable as she is, and too used to it — but no one seems to realise this. Least of all Rudolph, who'd like to fulfil her slightest wish.' She pressed her lips together and fell silent.

At that moment, the doorbell rang.

'That must be my parents!' cried Tony.

Anna ran to the window. 'Goodnight, Tony,' she said, and flew off.

Tony went to the front door and opened it.

'Well Tony, have you had a happy time being bored?' asked his father as he took off his muddy shoes.

'Mmmm, you could say that,' said Tony.

29

His mother nodded complacently. 'If you'd come with us, you wouldn't have been bored. But then you always know better!'

Tony grinned happily. 'Yes, I always do know better!'

# 8

# A Spy in Love

On Monday evening, Tony went to his room straight after supper, even though there was an old cowboy film on television which even his parents wanted to watch. But Tony had told them he still had something to do for school. It was true enough: he had to get his English book back!

Once in his room, he opened the window and leaned out — and saw Anna.

She swooped towards him like a huge moth and landed on the window-sill.

'Hello, Tony,' she said, still a little out of breath.

'Hello,' he replied huskily.

She reached under her cloak and held out his English book and his pen. 'Here. I took a lot of trouble over it!'

'Thanks,' said Tony in embarrassment, wanting to look in the book.

But Anna cried: 'No! You may only read it when you're on your own. In any case, we two have something much better to do!' she added.

'Have we? But my parents are here!'

'Can't you make up an excuse? It'll only be for half an hour.'

'Where are we going?'

Anna giggled. 'To the park. Today is Olga's last practice lesson.'

'Will she have to find her own food from now on?'

'No. It's just that Aunt Dorothy wants to change the place where she gives her lessons. Things are gradually hotting up in the park.'

'What do you mean — hotting up?'

'Well — Olga's acting in such a stupid bungling way that it's made passers-by and the park attendants curious about them more than once already — but you'll see for yourself in a moment. What's more, Rudolph will be there too.'

'Rudolph?' At the thought of the Little Vampire, Tony's voice took on a happier note. 'Is he giving Olga lessons too?'

'No,' Anna answered, laughing behind her hand. 'On the contrary, Aunt Dorothy has strictly forbidden him to be there. Otherwise Olga concentrates even more badly on her lessons.'

'So now he's watching secretly?'

'Yes. A spy in love!' Anna laughed so loudly that Tony was afraid his parents might hear.

'Not so loud!' he warned.

'Are you coming then?' she asked in a whisper. 'You've still got Uncle Theodore's cloak.'

Tony hesitated. But the prospect of spying on Olga's lesson and perhaps even meeting the Little Vampire was very appealing. 'What if Aunt Dorothy sees us?'

'I'm sure she won't,' Anna assured him. 'She'll be much too busy.'

'All right then,' declared Tony. 'I'll just let my parents know.'

'You won't tell them, will you?' asked Anna distrustfully.

'No of course not. I've already got an idea what I'll tell them . . . but you must take the cloak.'

With his English book in his hand, he made for the door. 'Wait for me down below.'

Ten minutes later, Tony came out of the block. He made his way slowly along the paved path and looked carefully around him — but he could not see Anna anywhere.

Suddenly someone covered his eyes from behind. Tony gave a yell and turned round. It was Anna.

'Oh, it's you!' he said in relief.

'Did it work with your parents?' she asked.

'Yes. I told them I was going to Olly to talk about the essay.' He pointed to the English book, which he had stuck in the belt of his trousers, with a grin.

'Did they believe you?'

'Of course. If it's anything to do with school work . . . ! But they said I mustn't stay out too long.'

'Okay, come on then, let's hurry,' said Anna giving him the second cloak. Tony put it on and off they flew.

After a while, the park came into view below them. Tony could make out the large sun-bathing area and the paddling pool. All around the paddling pool stood swings and slides and climbing frames, looking like weird prehistoric monsters. Tony looked anxiously over at the tall trees.

'Can you see Olga and Aunt Dorothy?' he called softly.

'No,' whispered Anna. 'They're hiding behind the toilets.'

'Who on earth is going to come walking past there?'

Anna giggled. 'Oh, people who've got caught short: walkers, children carrying paper lanterns, joggers. . . .'

She pointed to a man in a tracksuit and gleaming white trainers. 'There look! A long-distance runner! Come on, let's hide in that big tree over there,' she whispered and headed for a huge oak tree.

Tony followed and landed next to her in the fork of a branch. They watched with bated breath as the man ran round the paddling pool and approached the hut with the toilets in it.

Tony had just asked: 'Where's Rudolph?' when a husky voice above them answered: 'Try looking up here!'

Tony almost fell off the branch with fright. He looked up and saw the Little Vampire. 'Rudolph, it's you!' he said happily.

'Yes,' hissed the vampire, nodding to him briefly. 'But don't disturb me: I've got to be on the look-out. . . .'

'You're not very nice to your best friend,' remarked Anna.

The vampire made no reply. Tense and strained, he stared in the direction of the toilet hut. 'Now!' he murmured. 'Go get him, Olga!'

Involuntarily Tony winced. But of course the words were not directed at him but at the man in the tracksuit who had just disappeared unsuspectingly into the toilets.

Tony held his breath — what on earth was going to happen now?

A small figure in a black cloak came out from behind the hut and went hesitantly over to the door. That must be Olga! She wore something light on her head, but what it was, Tony could not see. Would she go in?

No! Just then, the man came out again. Olga stepped over to him, raised her arms menacingly — and the man began to laugh! He laughed so loudly you could hear it all round the playground! Then he turned round and simply ran off, leaving behind him a totally bewildered Olga.

'What a bum!' fumed the vampire. 'He could at least have been frightened! If it goes on like this, Olga will never develop her self-confidence!'

'Huh, self-confidence!' said Anna. 'Olga's got more than enough of that!'

'You're just jealous!' retorted the vampire.

'Jealous of Olga? You must be joking! It just makes me mad to see how you let yourself be ordered around by her!'

'Me? Ordered around?'

'Yes, ordered around!' said Anna. 'You're just blinded by your crush on her and you don't even see what a selfish beast your beloved Olga is!'

'What did you say?' shrieked the Little Vampire. '*You* are the beast — you — you set of baby milk teeth!'

Tony's whole body was trembling: surely Aunt Dorothy could not help hearing all this noise! And he was right. As Anna and Rudolph went on fighting fast and furiously, a large dark shape appeared in front of the toilet hut and gazed over at them.

'For heaven's sake! It's Aunt Dorothy!' Tony piped. Anna and Rudolph fell silent — but it was too late.

Aunt Dorothy's voice rang out shrilly over the empty playground. 'Rudolph? Is it you hiding up there in that tree?'

'Yes, Aunt Dorothy,' answered the Little Vampire in a plaintive voice.

'And you're not alone, are you?' she asked piercingly.

'A-Anna's with me,' stuttered the vampire.

'I wanted to stop him spying on you,' called Anna.

'Be off with you! At once!' scolded Aunt Dorothy. 'And don't let me see you again!'

'No, Aunt Dorothy, we're going!' called the Little Vampire.

Anna and Tony exchanged looks.

'Don't leave me in the lurch!' implored Tony.

Anna smiled at him encouragingly. 'I'll come back,' she said softly. Then she and Rudolph flew away, leaving Tony all alone.

He hardly dared breathe in case he gave himself away. A couple of minutes passed which seemed like an eternity. Why was Aunt Dorothy still standing in front of the toilets? Did she suspect there was still someone in the tree? If she came over, he was done for! He thought of how she could hypnotise a person just by looking at them. . . .

Suddenly, through the trees on the other side of the paddling pool, Tony saw something gleaming, and immediately three lads stepped out of the shadow of the trees and made their way over to the toilet hut. Tony felt a weight fall off him: so Aunt Dorothy had not been interested in him, after all, but in the three lads! One of them was holding a torch which he switched on every now and then. Now he directed the beam on the toilet shed, to the exact spot where Aunt Dorothy had been standing a moment before — but she had disappeared. At that moment, someone touched Tony on the shoulder. He jumped. To his huge relief, he saw Anna crouching next to him. 'Come on, quick!' she whispered. 'While Aunt Dorothy is still behind the hut!'

Tony was only too pleased to leave his hiding place and follow her. Once in the air, he said: 'Poor Olga! She certainly won't have any luck with those three!'

'What did you say?' spat Anna. 'Are you on Olga's side too, now?'

'N-no,' he assured her quickly.

'It started just like this with Rudolph!' she said grimly. 'First he felt sorry for her and wanted to help her — and then he tumbled helplessly into her net.'

'What net?'

'That's just an expression. Olga weaves a snare around you till you do exactly what she wants.'

Tony looked at her and did not know what to say. But he had to say something so as to reassure her. . . .

As they said goodbye, he remarked: 'You really don't need to worry about Olga. I'll stick with you.'

'Thanks,' she said and smiled faintly. Then she flew away.

Tony went into the house and pressed the lift call button.

# 9

# Anna's Essay

In the lift, he suddenly noticed he was still wearing the vampire cloak. In a fever, he pulled it off and tried to fold it, which was not at all easy in the narrow little compartment. But he did manage it and when the lift stopped, he had hidden it under his sweater.

He opened the door of the flat with sweating hands. He could hear men's voices talking loudly, and gave a sigh of relief: that meant the film was still on. With any luck his parents would not have had a chance to think about how long he had been out!

'Have you finished your essay?' called his mother, as he walked past the living room.

'Yes,' he answered and went on quickly.

Once in his room, he had just stuffed the musty smelling cloak into the bottom drawer of his desk when his mother came into the room.

'Poof, what a stink!' she said, wrinkling her nose. 'Olly's parents must be heavy smokers!'

'Yes, they are,' said Tony, restraining a smile.

'And you really have been doing your homework?'

'Of course.'

'May I read the essay?'

Tony went white. 'Why?'

'You know quite well how many careless mistakes you always make.'

'I — I haven't this time,' Tony tried to put her off. But it was no good.

'I don't believe it!' she declared. 'If you do your homework so late in the evening, you're bound to make even more mistakes than usual.'

'Okay, then,' sighed Tony and, resigned to his fate, he pulled the English book out from the top of his trousers. It had got a kink in it but otherwise it looked quite reasonable.

'The way you treat your things...' scolded his mother.

'What do you mean?' asked Tony. 'That hasn't hurt my trousers!'

'But look at the book!' said his mother crossly and went out of the room.

I do hope Anna's written something sensible! thought Tony.

But it did not look as if his wish was to be granted, for after only a few moments, his mother was back, and she seemed to be more than a little angry!

'Tony, come in here! We must have a talk with you!' she declared.

'What about?' he pretended not to guess.

'You know very well what about.'

'I don't!'

'Oh don't you? The next thing you'll say is that you didn't even write the essay yourself!'

'Exactly — ' growled Tony — she would never believe him. . . .

With mixed feelings, he trotted behind her into the living room. His father was sitting on the sofa holding Tony's English book. He pointed to an armchair. 'Sit down.'

'No thanks,' answered Tony, 'I'd prefer to stand.'

'All right.' His father cleared his throat as if he were going to make a speech, and began: 'What I want to be when I grow up. I would like to be a vampire, because I think that vampires aren't basically bad creatures, like it's said in most books and films, but that it all depends on their characters (like with humans) whether they are "good" or "bad". I think there would be lots of advantages in being a vampire, like eternal life and being able to fly. Mankind has always dreamed of that and I have too. I just think it would be brill to be a vampire. I'm sure I could cope with any problems there might be in being a vampire, especially if I had a vampire girlfriend at my side — for love can overcome all problems.'

While his father was reading this out, Tony tried to keep his expression calm, which was not very easy, especially since he did not know what was in the essay either. But Anna's last sentence took his breath away and even his ears went red.

'Don't you realise what hair-raising nonsense you've written?' asked his mother, who had been watching him closely.

42

'I . . . it was meant to be a joke!' stuttered Tony.

'A joke?' She picked up the book and waved it about in the air in a frenzy. 'But this is homework!'

'Olly and I — we made a bet.'

'A bet?'

'He said he'd give me 70 pence if I wrote about wanting to be a vampire.'

'And you were stupid enough to take on this bet?' cried Tony's father heatedly.

'Well, yes, I mean 70 pence is — '

'For a measly 70 pence you'd risk getting a bad mark!' exclaimed his mother. 'I suppose you hadn't thought what your teacher was going to say about all this!'

'No,' he answered, truthfully enough.

'Well — you will now rewrite the essay.'

'Now?'

'Yes.'

'But you said yourself that you shouldn't do homework as late as this.'

His parents exchanged looks.

'Well, tomorrow afternoon then,' declared Mum. 'And you can tell your teacher you are rewriting it.' In a more conciliatory voice she added: 'I must admit, your handwriting has improved. This time you really made an effort to be neat and tidy. You ought to keep it up.'

'Oh really?' murmured Tony, turning his head away. 'May I go now?'

'Yes. Goodnight.'

Once in his room, Tony read Anna's piece through once more: '. . . for love can overcome all problems.'

Certainly not *all* problems! he thought, because tomorrow morning in school he would have to admit he had not done the essay. . . .

# 10

# Finished and Done With

The following day, it was already getting
dark and Tony was still sitting at his desk.
In front of him lay the clean new exercise
book which his mother had given him so
that his teacher would not read the wrong
— Anna's! — essay by mistake.

'What I want to be when I grow up. . . .'
What a stupid subject! Why should he have
to choose a career so soon? He had read in
the newspaper that you should be thankful
if you managed to get a place at college even!
In any case, Anna's essay wasn't that bad at
all! he thought, as he stared at the blank
pages. He would have loved to have seen
his teacher's expression if she had read it!

But Tony did not actually want to be a
vampire — even if Anna wanted it as much
as ever. The business with the vampire
dummy had shown that all too clearly.
Anna and her vampire teeth. . . .

Suddenly Tony had an idea what he
would write.

I would like to be a dentist, he wrote. I
would like to have a large practice and
patients who did not always shout 'Ouch!'
when it hurt a bit. I would have two treat-
ment rooms. I would paint one of them
green, because green calms you down, and
one of them red, because red makes you

feel happy. I would treat anxious patients in the green room and unhappy ones in the red room. I would buy myself only the very best drills. While I was drilling away, I would play cheerful music. . . .

Tony stopped. That must be enough, surely?

An excited knocking on the window made him jump. He looked up and saw two figures dressed in black sitting on the window-sill: Anna, who gave him a friendly smile, and the Little Vampire. Rudolph seemed to be in a great hurry, because he knocked on the pane again.

'Okay, I'm coming,' said Tony. He went to the door and turned the key in the lock, before opening the window.

'Have you got the cloak?' asked Rudolph coming straight to the point and jumping into the room in one bound.

Anna slipped more gracefully down from the window-sill. 'Good evening, Tony,' she said.

'Hi,' murmured Tony, rather confused by this sudden visit from the pair of them.

'Well, where is it?' growled the vampire, looking round inquiringly.

'What?'

'Uncle Theodore's cloak,' explained Anna. 'We need it — for Olga. She had a mishap with her own cloak yesterday evening.'

'A mishap, you call it?' retorted the vampire heatedly. 'She was in mortal danger!'

'Not so loud!' objected Tony imploringly. 'My parents are in the living room.'

'Your parents? In the living room?' the vampire gave a startled look towards the door.

'I've locked it,' Tony reassured him. 'But even so, we must be quiet.'

'Okay,' agreed the vampire, and with a lower voice he asked, 'So, where have you put it?'

'Don't go on at Tony so!' interrupted Anna. 'I'm sure first he'd like to know what happened to Olga's cloak. Wouldn't you, Tony?'

Tony nodded.

'All right by me,' growled the vampire, sitting down on Tony's bed.

It struck Tony that he looked even more pale than usual. His eyes were red and he seemed thin and wasted. The saying: 'Love brings roses to your cheeks!' was certainly not true in the Little Vampire's case!

'So what did happen to the cloak?' asked Tony.

'Olga was caught by three tough yobbos,' said the vampire darkly.

'So she says!' retorted Anna, laughing spitefully.

'And were you there to see, by any chance?' Rudolph asked angrily.

'No, but Aunt Dorothy was. And she told me what really happened.'

'I can't wait to hear about it!' said Rudolph sarcastically.

'Olga and Aunt Dorothy were trying to creep up on the three lads from behind,'

47

Anna told them. 'But Olga spoiled every-thing by her noisy tramping. The boys got suspicious, turned round, one of them switched on his torch, and Olga and Aunt Dorothy were dazzled and had to escape — and as they did so, Olga and her cloak got tangled up in some brambles.'

'Huh!' went the vampire. 'It was all com-pletely and totally different. I know, because Olga told me — and Olga doesn't lie!'

'Oh really?' was all Anna would say, looking meaningfully at the ceiling.

'Yes! Without any provocation, three yobs attacked her — *three* of them — tore her cloak and pulled her hair. One of them pinched her hair-slide — Olga's favourite hair-slide, the last present her father gave her. . . .' The Little Vampire gave a sob.

'Oh how moving!' Anna said bitingly. 'And what about the cloak?'

'Torn, ripped to shreds!' The vampire wrung his hands.

'You're exaggerating again,' said Anna dryly. 'It only had a couple of holes which can easily be sewn up again.'

'Yes, but that will take time. If only I knew how to darn. . . .' The vampire's voice took on an adoring tone. 'I would lay Olga's cloak over my knee, and carefully pull the thread through the dark material for hour upon hour. . . .' He gave a deep sigh.

'Perhaps Aunt Dorothy will show you how to do it,' growled Anna. 'Then you can start a sewing group — for your beloved Olga!'

48

'Huh!' said the vampire and stuck out his tongue at Anna. For the first time Tony saw a vampire tongue: it was very long and dark red. He shuddered.

'I — er, you'll want the cloak straight away then,' he stuttered. 'Just a m-moment, it's in my desk.'

He opened the drawer and pulled out the cloak from behind some books.

At that moment, there were steps in the hallway.

The Little Vampire snatched up the cloak, jumped onto the window-sill and flew off without another word.

Anna said hastily: 'See you soon, Tony,' and followed him.

'Tony, why have you locked your door?' he heard his mother ask. 'Open up!'

'Coming,' he answered and deliberately slowly crossed over to the door.

His mother was standing outside, red in the face. 'Since when have you locked the door of your room?' she asked heatedly. 'You know we don't like you to! No one here in the flat locks doors, Dad doesn't, I don't — we don't keep secrets from one another — or do we?' she asked, suddenly suspicious. 'It smells of burning!'

'It was my head!' said Tony. 'It started to smoke — too much thinking!'

His mother looked at him disbelievingly. Then her gaze fell on the exercise book. 'Have you finished?' she asked.

'Yes,' he growled, 'finished and done with!'

She laughed, and began to read: '"I would like to be a dentist. I would like to have a large practice. . . ." Well, well,' she exclaimed in relief. 'At long last, not a word about vampires!'

# 11

# The Peabody Vault

On Saturday afternoon Tony asked his father: 'Could you help me? I want to build something in my room.'

'Build something? What?'

'A den. And I need to turn my bed round to do it.'

'That really will be some den!' remarked his dad with a laugh.

'I'll also need blankets,' said Tony. 'Preferably black ones so that it will be nice and dark.'

'We haven't got any black blankets,' his mother said. 'But I have got some old black material in a cupboard.'

'Oh, yes please!' Tony was delighted.

If only his parents knew what they were helping him with: that evening, at quarter past eight, there was a film on television called 'The Dance of the Vampires' and he wanted to turn his room into a vault to watch it! But he wouldn't tell them till later — just before they set off to the cinema. And there was a great deal to do before then. . . .

At half past seven, there was a knock on the door of his room.

'Tony?' called his mother. 'We're just going. May we come and see your den?'

'Yes, come on in,' he called happily and sat down on his desk, which he had turned into a coffin with black material and a cardboard cross which he had wrapped round with silver foil.

Curious, not knowing what to expect, his parents came into the room — and came to a halt as if they had been struck by lightning. They were certainly not prepared for the sight which awaited them!

'The Peabody Vault' they read, in blood red letters on a sign which was fixed to the cord of the light which hung from the ceiling. Tony had painted larger than life-size vampire heads and hung them on the walls. There was nothing to be seen of the furniture: Tony had draped it all with black material. But the most gruesome thing of all was his upturned bed: Tony had suspended a black cloth over the four feet, and under it a lying figure was visible, motionless as a corpse. . . .

Tony's mother gave a cry. 'Who's under there?'

He grinned. 'No one. Just my bedclothes!'

'You didn't half give me a fright!'

'Really?' said Tony, proud of the effect he had created with his bedclothes. 'Watch this, I'm going to turn out the light. . . .'

He quickly switched on his torch and lay down next to the 'corpse'. Then he pressed the light switch. Now all you could see was the feeble glow of the torch shimmering through the black material — and it was so spooky that even Tony found he had goose-pimples!

'Eeeugh! This is frightful!' cried his mother.

'Isn't it?' said Tony happily.

'But there is one thing that shouldn't be in a vault,' remarked Dad.

'What's that?'

'The television!'

Of course, Tony had not draped a black cloth over the television. What was the point, since he was about to switch it on?

'Or do you think vampires have a power supply in their vault?' grinned Dad.

Tony was irritated by his father's superior tone of voice. Cheekily he retorted, 'Why should they? They don't need one. You can get televisions which run on batteries, you know!'

His father laughed. 'What a marvellous thought! Vampires looking at the News broadcast!'

'Why not?' said Tony. 'When you think of how much blood is shown flowing every evening. . . .'

'I know why Tony hasn't covered the television!' his mother said suddenly. 'There's probably another of these terrible horror films on.'

Tony had to smile. 'That's right. Tonight they're showing "The Dance of the Vampires". It's my favourite film.'

'What time?' she asked suspiciously.

'Quarter past eight,' answered Tony with relish.

'As early as that?'

'Yes. Watch it with me. It's a fantastic film.'

'No thanks,' she replied and made the sort of face you make when you've bitten into a lemon. 'We prefer to go to the cinema and see a worthwhile film.'

'An even more worthwhile one, you mean?' said Tony, grinning like the Cheshire cat.

'Just take care you don't get bitten,' re-marked Dad as he said goodbye.

'Bitten? What by?'

'Your vampires!'

# 12

# 'The Dance of the Vampires'

Tony was just about to switch on the television when he heard an extraordinary noise at the window. It sounded as though an enormous bird had crashed against it.

He pulled the curtain aside and looked straight into the small white face of a vampire he had never seen before. It had to be a girl because it had a red slide in its hair. Perhaps it was — Olga? Now it was motioning him to open the window. With shaking hands, Tony did so, and the vampire girl climbed into his room.

'Are you Tony?' She had a powerful, husky voice and was almost as tall as he was.

'Y-yes,' he stuttered.

'I am the Honourable Olga Pigsbubble,' she declared. 'So this is where you live. . . .'

As she gazed curiously around, Tony took a good look at her. For a vampire, she looked pretty good: she had little freckles on a snub nose, big blue eyes and her hair was brushed carefully. The only thing that was slightly disturbing was the strong smell of decay.

Olga had noticed his look. 'Do you like the look of me?' she asked.

Tony went bright red. 'Yes — '

She smiled with satisfaction. 'I thought

you did. I like your room,' she went on.
'We had paintings on the walls of the vault
at home.' She pointed to the painted vampire heads. 'Did you do those?'

'Yes,' nodded Tony.

'Would you like to paint me?' she asked
eagerly, striking an affected pose right in
front of Tony. 'Back at home in Transylvania,
I often had my portrait painted.'

'I — I don't know exactly where my
pencils are at the moment,' Tony murmured.

Olga's face took on an irritated expression. The sweet smile vanished, and Tony
caught sight of her pointed vampire teeth.

'Of course, I could look for them, if you
like,' he said hastily.

'No!' she said sharply. 'I don't feel like
being painted any more.' With that, she
turned round and went over to the window.

'W-wait!' called Tony.

She stopped and looked at him expectantly. 'Yes?'

'Does Aunt Dorothy know you are here?'

'No. She's back in the vault, darning.'

'How did you find my window?'

She laughed huskily. 'Quite simple. I
begged Rudolph to show me. At first he
didn't want to. But as he cannot refuse me
anything for long, he finally agreed. And
he was quite right after all,' she continued.
'You are really nice. I'm sure we'll be friends!
But now I must fly — Rudolph's waiting for
me in the chestnut tree.'

She gave him a smile and climbed up

onto the window-sill. Then she spread out her arms — and let them fall again in surprise. 'You? What are you doing here?' she cried.

An icy shudder ran through Tony. What if Aunt Dorothy was sitting outside his open window? But it wasn't Aunt Dorothy. . . .

'Yes, it's me,' he heard Anna reply. 'And I've heard everything!'

Her voice sounded full of menace, but Olga was not impressed.

'So?' was all she said. 'It's not forbidden to tell Tony that he's nice! Especially when it's quite true,' she added, and without deigning to waste another word on Anna, she flew off.

Anna stormed furiously into the room. 'So she's done it to you, now, too, has she?'

'Done what?'

'Twisted you round her little finger!' she cried. 'And from what I can see, she's managed it extremely successfully. You've even re-arranged your room for her!'

Tony could hardly believe his ears. 'For Olga? But — '

Anna would not let him finish. 'You don't have to explain. I understand. Farewell!'

And before Tony could stop her, she disappeared.

He stood transfixed, not knowing what to think. First the unexpected visit from Olga — then the confrontation with Anna — her groundless jealousy — and finally her goodbye, as though they would never see one another again. . . .

He closed the window and switched on the television. A fat, sweaty man was singing: 'I'm just so-o lonely'. Tony felt exactly the same: alone in a vault, with parents who were out having fun in the cinema, a friend who didn't want any more to do with him, and a girlfriend who'd just given him the boot —

Suddenly he hated all the black material draped everywhere, the grimacing vampire faces, the silver cross, and like some wild animal, he began to tear everything down again.

When he had finished, he felt much better. He sat down and began to watch the television. A group of people in national dress were doing a dance — and at that moment, he remembered 'The Dance of the Vampires', which he had quite forgotten about in all the uproar.

He quickly switched channels. He watched as the owner of the village inn transported his coffin into Dracula's castle. But it was odd — the pleasant tingling of nerves which he usually felt when he watched a vampire film refused to come. Again and again, all he could think of was Anna.

His bad mood was still with him the following morning.

'"The Dance of the Vampires" was obviously a bit too much for you!' teased Dad. 'You still look quite exhausted!'

Tony had to grin in spite of himself. 'That's right. The dance I had with the vampires was really too much for me.'

Of course his parents did not understand the joke, and merely looked at him in surprise. Tony's mother poured out some coffee.

'There's one thing I am pleased about,' she said.

'What's that?' asked Tony.

'Your room. Thank God that dreadful vault has gone.'

'Not just the vault . . . ' sighed Tony.

## 13

# Postman

The week passed without Tony hearing anything from either Rudolph or Anna. On Saturday evening, he sat in his room, leafing through various horror stories — and waited. But no one knocked on the window.

He had to do something. But what? If Anna had been an ordinary girl, he could have given her a letter in the school playground, or telephoned her, or simply gone round to see her. But as she wasn't. . . .

What if he left a message for her near the vault? He remembered the two clay vampires he had made in the pottery class. They were hollow — he could hide a note for Anna inside one of them. Yes, it was a brill idea! He took one of the figures down from the shelf. Then, on a piece of paper, he wrote:

Dear Anna,
I must talk to you. I am sorry about Olga, really I am.
Tony.

The following afternoon, he would go to the cemetery and leave the figure in a likely place!

The next day was cold and grey — just

right for Tony, because not so many people would be out and about in such weather. Immediately after lunch he set out on his bicycle. He had put the clay figure and the letter under his jacket.

He went to the main entrance and locked up his bicycle. Then he opened the gates. The cemetery lay deserted before him like a great big peaceful garden. You could almost feel the caring, tending hand of the Nightwatchman — and of his assistant gardener, Sniveller. With a shudder, Tony realised McRookery had got reinforcements!

He looked around anxiously, but neither was to be seen. They were probably taking their mid-day break over in McRookery's house, which was hidden behind some tall bushes. Tony could only make out the red roof and the chimney, out of which a thin plume of smoke rose. Perhaps they were sitting round the fire sharpening their stakes. . . .

Tony quickened his step. He passed a freshly dug grave where someone was obviously about to be buried — how spooky! Close by, there was a grave simply covered in flowers. 'Rest in peace' was engraved in gold letters on a black polished stone.

Brrr! Recent graves always gave him the creeps. He walked on quickly and was pleased to reach the rear part of the cemetery at last. With a beating heart, he caught sight of the tall tree. No one would guess that underneath it was the entrance to the vault.

Not even McRookery knew about it, even though he spent every spare moment snuffling around for vampires. He was still looking for single vampire graves, and for that reason, the Sackville-Baggs had long since moved their coffins into a communal vault. Now only the heart-shaped headstones, which still lay here and there in the grass, were left to show that there had once been vampire graves in this part of the cemetery.

Tony strode slowly through the knee-high grass, on the lookout for the headstones. After a while, he stumbled against a crumbling, heart-shaped stone. With difficulty, he deciphered the inscription:

Dorothy Sackville-Bagg-Pigsbubble
1807–1851

Tony gulped. It would be Aunt Dorothy's! Hastily, he went on farther.

He found the headstones of Anna's parents, her grandparents and her uncle. But he could not find the ones belonging to the vampire children. So was it really true that they did not have headstones? Tony had already looked for them in vain once before.

Suddenly his glance fell on a rectangular slab. He picked it up and saw it had an inscription. Excitedly he began to pick away the thick layer of moss. His trouble was rewarded for he read:

63

Anna Sackville-Bagg
1842–

and underneath:

We are waiting for you
for ever and ever.

So that was it! thought Tony in relief.

Anna certainly did not have such a splendid stone as her relations, but even so, someone had thought of her!

'We are waiting for you' — to whom did that refer? Her parents? Presumably they had died before Anna, for they had only been able to give the year of her birth and not the date of her death.

He made sure once more that no one was watching him. Then he placed Anna's stone against the heart-shaped headstone of her mother and hid the pottery figure behind it. He gave a sigh of relief and studied his handiwork. He was certain the other vampires would not notice the change. Anna would be the only one to realise that someone had stood her little rectangular stone upright. And then, surely, she would be curious and would look more closely, and then she would discover his letter. . . .

Well done! Tony gave himself a pat on the back and made his way happily back to the gates.

# 14

# McRookery's House

When he saw the red roof of McRookery's house, Tony had a sudden urge to take a look at the signboard Anna had told him about. Did it really say 'Sniveller: Assistant Gardener' on it?

He left the main path and turned down a narrow side alley. Hidden by the tall hedges, he approached the house slowly, with a pleasant tingling feeling in his tummy. After all, nothing could happen to him, for he had hidden the clay figure and it wasn't against the law to go for a walk in the cemetery.

After a while, the path turned a bend, and suddenly Tony found himself in front of McRookery's garden gate. Startled, he stared over at the house. It was quite different from what he had imagined. He had thought that a nightwatchman of a cemetery would live in a dilapidated gloomy ruin of a house, the very sight of which would be enough to freeze the blood in your veins. But McRookery's house looked almost inviting: it was built of red brick, had green shutters at the windows and a rosebush was in full bloom by the front door. What was more, Tony could see no signboard anywhere — there was only a little pane of glass set in the door. And behind the pane of glass . . . something was moving!

Then all at once the door opened and a tall lanky man came out carrying a rubbish bin. Tony just had time to dart to safety behind a thick bush, from where he watched as the man came down the garden path. Just a few steps from Tony, he flipped open the lid of a dustbin and tipped out the contents of the bin he was carrying. He did not seem to have the slightest suspicion that someone was watching him, for his face was relaxed and he was humming to himself.

So that's what Sniveller looks like! thought Tony, quite fancying himself as a detective. Sniveller had yellowy blond hair, a great beaked nose and a wispy blond moustache. His eyes were rather pink, like a rabbit's. His hands were unusual: huge, with carefully manicured long nails.

Luckily Sniveller turned and went back to the house. The door was still open and Tony was able to have a quick glance into the hall. And what he saw took his breath away: in a basket stood long, sharp wooden stakes ready to hand; and on the wall hung a large crucifix, around which was draped a string of garlic cloves.

Brrr! Tony shuddered. He ran a couple of steps bent double, then stood upright and raced to the gates.

# 15

# A Midnight Visit

That night Tony dreamed about a letter which he had to deliver to an old house. He rang at the front door, but no one opened it. So then he ran all round the house, knocking on the windows. He knocked and knocked. ... Suddenly Tony awoke with a jump. The loud knocking was not in his dream — someone was knocking on his window. It must be Anna!

He jumped out of bed, pulled the curtains aside and flung open the window. But it was not Anna sitting outside. The Little Vampire was perched on the window-sill with an embarrassed smile on his face.

'Hello, Tony,' he said in his husky voice.

'Rudolph!' stuttered Tony.

'Nice surprise for you, isn't it?' remarked the vampire, and climbed into the room.

Tony switched on the lamp on his desk. 'I — was already asleep,' he murmured.

'So I see,' said the vampire, pointing to Tony's rumpled bed. 'But never mind! You can go back to sleep straight away — once we've discussed this business of a Transylvanian Evening.'

'A what?'

'We want to celebrate on Saturday. Are your parents in?'

'My parents?' Tony peered at his alarm

clock. It was just after midnight. 'Yes. But I'm sure they're asleep.'

The vampire snorted indignantly. 'I don't mean now — I mean on Saturday, when we celebrate with a Transylvanian Evening.'

'I think they're going out to the cinema.'

'Great.' The vampire looked pleased and rubbed his hands. 'Have you any eggs?'

'Eggs?' Tony was completely nonplussed. 'Yes — '

'Then that's everything fixed for Saturday.'

'But — I don't even know what a Transylvanian Evening is!'

The vampire gave him a friendly grin. 'You'll find out soon enough.'

'And I don't know where you're going to hold it either!'

'Don't you?'

'No.'

The vampire gave a broad grin, so Tony could see his pointed eye-teeth. 'Here.'

'What?'

'It's all because of Olga,' explained the vampire. 'She's terribly homesick for Transylvania.'

'But what's that got to do with me?'

'Olga told us that your room looked like the Pigsbubble family vault.'

'Oh I see,' said Tony. 'I changed it all around. But it was a heck of a lot of work.'

'I'm sure you could do it all again for Olga,' the vampire replied, adding in a choking voice: 'The poor thing. Every evening she just lies in her coffin and cries.'

He wiped his eyes and climbed onto the window-sill. 'So, see you Saturday, Tony!'

'Wait!' cried Tony.

'What is it?'

'Will Anna be coming too?'

'Yes. Providing her graze is better by then.'

'Is she hurt?' Tony was startled.

The vampire giggled. 'She must have been very worked up after she called on you last Saturday. Anyway, apparently she flew into the branch of a tree and got a long scratch on her face. And she's so vain she doesn't want to be seen in public looking like that.'

'Oh, I see,' said Tony. Then perhaps she was not cross with him any more and simply had not visited him because of the scratch?

Once back in bed, he was much too excited to fall asleep at once. Who knew what a Translyvanian Evening might entail — and Anna might even come. . . .

16

# Party Preparations

At lunch the following day, Tony tried to find out what his mother thought of parties. Sounding as casual as possible, he said: 'By the way, Sebastian had a party on Friday.'

'Oh?' was all she said, twisting her spaghetti round her fork.

'Yes. And he said it was brill.'

'Ah.'

'Would you ever let me have one?'

'Have what?'

'Have a party here.'

'I'd have to discuss it with your father.'

'But you're always going on at me about finding more friends. And Sebastian said it's easy to make friends if you have a party.'

'Who would you invite then?'

'Olly, Sebastian — '

'No girls?'

'Yes, of course. Anna, Olga — '

'Olga — now that's a name I haven't heard before. Is she new in your class?'

'Fairly. She's foreign.'

'Oh? Where does she come from?'

'Trans —' Tony bit his lip. 'Rumania.' Rumania sounded a good deal less dangerous!

'If I know you, you've already got a date in mind.'

'Saturday,' Tony admitted, embarrassed. 'If that's okay with you.'

'We'll have to see what Dad says.'

'I'm sure Dad won't mind,' said Tony. And he was right.

That evening, his father went in for jokes. 'Ah, so Romeo's planning a party for his Juliet!' But he did give Tony £5. 'So you can buy some crisps and fizzy drink.'

Tony found it difficult not to laugh. He could guarantee that the vampires would not appreciate fizzy drink and crisps in the least! Olly and Sebastian might, but he did not intend to invite them.

Even so, on Saturday morning Tony supplied himself with five bottles of black-currant juice — it was nice and red — and two packets of peanuts and crisps. After all, his parents must not get suspicious!

Then he tried to decide whether he should turn his room back into a vault. It would be fun to ... but he did not want Anna or Rudolph to think he would dance to Olga's tune, so he contented himself with merely fixing the vampire faces on the walls. His mother was not at all pleased about that. 'You could at least make your room look a bit more festive!' she said reproachfully.

Tony grinned. 'Like it was two weeks ago — with the corpse?'

'For heaven's sake, no!' she said irritatedly. 'But you could bring up the streamers from the basement store.'

'Those old things!'

'Or you could hang up some balloons.'

'Have you got some?' he asked evasively.

'Yes. In the kitchen cupboard.'

'Oh, I don't know.' He did not like his mother interfering with his party preparations one bit! So he said: 'Parties are put on quite differently nowadays. But I suppose you haven't a clue about that!'

As he had expected, she pursed her lips angrily and went to the door. 'I only want the best for you,' she said, shutting the door behind her.

'The best for me?' grinned Tony. 'Who doesn't?'

# 17

# Off to the Transylvanian Evening!

At last, at half past seven, his parents said goodbye. From the kitchen window, Tony watched as they climbed into the car and drove away.

'That was lucky!' he sighed. Right up to the last moment he had been afraid they might change their minds and stay at home out of curiosity! He took a bottle of juice from the fridge and went back to his room. As a precaution, he opened the window — and found himself face to face with the Little Vampire.

'Hi, Tony!' said the vampire jumping down from the window-sill. He was obviously in the best of moods for he held out a bony hand to Tony and asked in his throaty voice: 'How are you?'

'F-fine!' stuttered Tony, startled by so much friendliness.

'Let's be off to the Transylvanian Evening!' cried the vampire and turned back to the window. 'You can come in!'

Olga appeared with a great big yellow bow in her hair, which jiggled up and down in a silly way.

'Hello, Tony!' she lisped, letting Rudolph help her down into the room. And as though she and the Little Vampire had both just

been on a course for good manners, she also asked: 'How are you?'

'Fine,' he answered, even more surprised. Perhaps it was going to turn into a fun evening. . . .

But all at once Olga's friendly expression altered. 'What's happened to your room?' she cried. 'It looks frightful!'

Tony grinned. 'Do you think so?'

'Yes. Where's the coffin? Where is the black material? Eeugh, what a common little room it is!'

Tony was secretly pleased she was upset, but of course he could not show it.

'All kids' rooms look like this,' he said innocently.

'They do not!' she contradicted violently. 'Last time I was here, it was quite different — like my beloved Pigsbubble vault,' she added, the corners of her mouth turning down as though she were about to cry.

This brought the Little Vampire into the battleground. 'Now Olga's miserable again,' he scolded. 'And all because of you — because you've changed your room round again. I even told you specifically not to!'

'Leave Tony alone, if you please!' said a clear voice from the window. Tony spun round and saw Anna sitting on the window-sill.

'You?' he murmured. 'I thought. . . .'

'. . . I wasn't coming any more, didn't you?' she finished the sentence for him. 'But I had to come — especially because of *her*,' she added, nodding in Olga's direction.

76

'Pooh!' said Olga, turning away scornfully.

Tony noticed a long red streak on Anna's cheek: her graze.

'That must have hurt,' he murmured softly.

'A bit,' she admitted, equally softly, and came into the room.

'Hey, what are you two whispering about over there?' cried the Little Vampire, adding pompously: 'We want to begin. Have you any music, Tony?'

'He's got a hi-fi,' said Olga, who was standing in front of Tony's bookshelves. With a giggle she began to press the knobs.

'Don't, you'll break it!' said Tony.

Olga looked offended and stepped back. 'Do it yourself then, spoilsport!'

Tony put in a cassette and loud pop music blared out.

'Haven't you got anything else?' asked Olga, looking cross.

'What do you want to listen to?'

'Folk music,' she answered, and in one swift movement, she swept off her cloak. Underneath she was wearing — a dirndl!

'It's our Transylvanian national costume,' she explained proudly.

Tony was speechless. With its frilly blouse, its embroidered bodice, gold buttons and full, knee-length skirt, she could have taken part in 'The Sound of Music'! Except that the clothes were all rather dusty.

'Pretty, isn't it?' she said, twirling in a circle. 'Actually, there's a little cap to go with it.'

'A cap?' remarked Anna cattily. 'But then we wouldn't be able to see your bow, and that would be such a pity!'

'You're just cross because you have to go around in a shabby old cloak and you haven't got a pretty dress like me!' retorted Olga. And with a glance at Tony, she added, 'And because Tony prefers well-dressed vampire girls to Cinderella types like you!'

Anna gave a piercing cry. 'You . . . !'

Hastily Tony said: 'I — er — like vampire cloaks,' and winked at Anna.

'Do you?' said Olga. 'Well, in that case — ' She grinned craftily and as fast as she had taken it off, she whipped the cloak back on again.

'But you looked prettier in that dress!' protested the Little Vampire. 'What's more, I wanted to ask Tony if he would lend me his leather breeches and Tyrolean hat. Then we'd make a great pair!'

Olga shook her head.

'You heard Tony say he prefers vampire cloaks — and after all, he is our host,' she added with a sugary sweet smile.

'One might think that you fancied Tony and not me!' remarked the vampire in a hurt voice.

Olga giggled. 'Well, I do,' she answered, studying Anna closely.

But Anna was not going to let herself be provoked this time. 'I'm sure Tony's got a thing or two to say about that!' she said calmly. 'And I don't believe that he would want a little wet like you as a girlfriend, who can't even take care of getting herself food!'

'A wet? I managed to bring my heavy coffin all the way here from Transylvania by myself!'

'Your folding coffin,' corrected Anna, 'which you simply strapped on your back.'

'But I did fly the whole way on my own!'

'Exactly!' exclaimed the Little Vampire. 'And now, leave Olga in peace, or you'll get it from me!'

'I think we ought to start the party,' suggested Tony.

Olga smiled graciously. 'As always, Tony is right.' She took a couple of tripping steps. 'I would so love to dance,' she said, 'but this music. . . .'

'I agree, the music is terrible,' the Little Vampire backed her up and addressed Tony in an imperious voice. 'Have you nothing more suitable?'

'You used to like this tape,' retorted Tony. 'You even asked me what band it was.'

'I did?' The vampire sounded amazed. Then he went on hastily, 'Well, maybe I did. My taste in music has improved recently — thanks to Olga!'

Anna laughed tartly. 'I didn't know it could be improved!'

The Little Vampire chose to ignore this remark. 'Have you any folk songs?' he asked Tony. 'Or military music?'

'I could see whether my parents have —'

'Oh yes!' cried Olga, clapping her hands happily.

'I'll be right back,' said Tony.

# 18

# A Great Big Vampire Boy Came Dancing up to Me!

As he was looking through his parents' records in the living room, Olga appeared.

'Have you found it?' she asked, looking round with obvious curiosity.

'What?'

'The folk music.'

Tony grinned and held up a record sleeve. 'The Deadnettleford Male Voice Choir sings Popular Country Melodies,' he read to her.

Olga nodded approvingly. 'Your parents obviously know about good music.'

At that moment, the Little Vampire came into the room.

'He's found a great record!' Olga cried. 'The Deadmen's Choir from Nettleford singing folk songs!'

'That sounds good,' said the vampire.

'They're not dead,' corrected Tony, 'but they don't sound much better than if they were!'

'Play it for us!' begged Olga.

'Here's an even better one: "The Huntsmen's Chorus of Upper Bogsbottom sings your Favourite Hunting Songs".'

The Little Vampire's expression darkened. 'Huntsmen? What do they hunt?'

'Partridges — '

'Birds? Huh!' dismissed the vampire.

'Otters — '

'Yuk!'

'Foxes — '

'Poof!'

'Rabbits, deer — '

'I bet they also hunt vampires,' said the Little Vampire darkly. 'Away with that record at once!' He tore it from Tony's hand and would probably have smashed it, if Anna had not stepped between them.

She took the record from him and gave it back to Tony. 'This belongs to his parents,' she declared, 'and we don't want Tony to get into trouble, do we?'

'No,' said the vampire in a small voice.

'I don't know why we keep fighting,' piped Olga. 'It must be because there is one person too many in this room. . . .' And she looked challengingly at Anna. But Anna was not to be ruffled.

'How right you are,' was all she said, looking Olga straight in the eye.

Tony quickly replaced the Huntsmen's Chorus on the shelf and showed the vampire another record.

'Here. My parents bought this one in Nether Bogsbottom too: "The Merry Village Warblers, under the leadership of Ernest Albert Rummage".'

'Who?' asked Olga delightedly. 'Scrummage?'

'Ernest Albert Rummage.'

'Rummage?' The vampire suddenly gave a loud roar, ran to the door and stood there trembling. 'But that's the village doctor who very nearly. . . .' Eyes wide in fear, he stared at the record sleeve which was still in Tony's hand.

'I didn't know that!' said Tony in embarrassment.

'Didn't know? But you were there!'

'But I couldn't know that Rummage was the leader of the choir!'

'Put that record away!' shrieked the vampire. 'I feel quite ill just looking at it!'

'No! I'd like to hear it!' said Olga sharply.

The vampire looked distraught. 'Rummage very nearly killed me — '

Olga shrugged her shoulders. 'So? Did he succeed? Well then, you've got no reason to get so worked up, have you?'

She turned to Tony with a winning smile. 'Do play it — just for me!'

Tony hesitated. 'I don't know. If Rudolph's got such horrible memories. . . .'

'That's a good reason to listen to it,' Olga broke in. 'My father, the Honourable Percy Pigsbubble, always said: "Inner resistance makes for strength".'

'What?' asked Anna.

'Inner resistance. You always have to do the things you hate most. For instance, going through a forest alone at night. In that way, you grow strong and fearless.'

Anna looked sympathetic. 'Your father said that?'

'He certainly did.'

'How very odd — Peculiar Percy Pigsbubble!'

'What did you call him?' exploded Olga. 'You have no right, even if his name is, er was, the Honourable Percy Pigsbubble.'

Anna smiled tolerantly. 'I wasn't talking about your father's name, I meant his methods of upbringing.'

'His what?'

'You must admit, he hasn't had the greatest success in the way he's brought you up. You certainly haven't turned out fearless and strong!'

The Little Vampire did not like that remark. 'Do stop laying into Olga all the time,' he snapped.

'Thank you,' said Olga, blowing him a kiss. 'May I now hear the record?'

The vampire gulped. Then, with obvious effort, he said: 'It's okay by me.'

'You are a treasure!' she trilled, and with a triumphant expression on her face, she went and sat down on the sofa. 'Play it, Tony!' she said, crossing her legs primly.

'Do what she says,' said Anna ironically. 'Olga's wish is our command!'

Olga gave her a daggered look but said nothing.

'I'll just play the first side,' Tony decided. 'My parents have actually forbidden me to have the party in the living room. On no account may any of you touch anything.'

'Okay,' answered Olga, lolling about on the sofa. 'Ah, this is cosy,' she enthused. 'Soft cushions instead of a rock hard coffin!'

In the meantime, Tony had put on the

record. Children's voices sang: 'The sun has got his hat on, hip-hip-hip-hooray . . . !'

The Little Vampire tightened his face in pain and winced as though he had indigestion.

'That's enough to give anyone a headache!' complained Anna.

Only Olga looked as though she liked the song. 'It's wonderful, quite wonderful!' she lied.

Luckily for the vampires it was only a short song. When it had finished, the full mixed choir began to sing: 'One night a great big bogey-man came dancing up to me, boom-boom!'

'A great big bogey-man! How sweet!' cried Olga, clapping her hands.

Even Rudolph's grumpy expression lightened and he began to hum the tune softly.

'He jumped up high, he bent down low, and threw his bag at me, boom-boom!' sang the choir.

'Come on, Rudolph, let's dance!' exclaimed Olga, jumping up from the sofa.

'Dance?' repeated the vampire in embarrassment, casting a furtive glance in Tony's direction. 'In front of the others?'

'Off we go!' cried Olga impatiently, taking his hands. As they danced, Olga sang along at the top of her voice — but with her own words: 'One night a great big vampire boy came dancing up to me, heh-heh! He jumped up high and bent down low and bared his teeth at me, heh-heh!'

After only a short time, Rudolph was quite red in the face. 'Stop!' he groaned.

'No, it's only just getting going!' she replied with a laugh, and danced even more wildly. At the words, 'He jumped up high and bent down low', she pushed Rudolph so violently that he stumbled against a standard lamp. The lamp fell over, and there was the sound of breaking glass.

# 19

# Friendship Stops at Blood!

'Oh no!' cried Tony. He ran over to try to pick it up — and collided with Anna who was also bending over the lamp. Her forehead cracked against his nose, which immediately began to bleed. Hastily he put a hand up to it.

Anna looked at him, and the tip of her tongue moved slowly across her lips. With a shudder, Tony remembered that she too had vampire teeth! But all at once, the expression in her eyes changed. Her look turned to one of concern and sympathy.

In some relief, he asked: 'Have you got a handkerchief?'

She nodded and pulled a large white rag out from under her cloak. It smelled disgusting when Tony pressed it against his nose, but the bleeding did begin to stop.

'Does it hurt?' she asked sympathetically.

'No.' He peered across at the other vampires. Olga was still trying to make Rudolph dance. He hung in her arms like some huge doll and let himself be pushed this way and that.

'Oh, it's no fun at all with you!' complained Olga, giving Rudolph a shove. He landed on the sofa. 'And the music is hopeless,' she grumbled, switching off the record player. 'What's that smell?' she asked suddenly. She cast a suspicious look in the direction of Anna and Tony. 'So appetising. . . .'

Now Rudolph began to take notice. He lifted his head and sniffed. A delighted smile spread over his face. 'It smells of blood!'

Tony pressed the handkerchief even harder against his nose. 'Blood? What on earth makes you think that?'

'What's wrong with your nose?' asked Olga tartly.

'My nose?' Feverishly Tony tried to think of an answer. 'I've got — er — hayfever!'

A frown appeared on Olga's face. She said in disbelief: 'So suddenly?'

'Yes,' nodded Tony. 'It's brought on by pollen which comes flying in when you least expect it.'

'Through a closed window?'

'No. It clings to your clothes. And then if you start leaping about' — here Tony had to smile as he remembered Olga's energetic dancing — 'It falls off again.'

Olga and Rudolph exchanged looks. Then the Little Vampire exclaimed: 'Shall I tell you what I think? You haven't got hayfever at all — you've got a nose-bleed!' With these last words, his voice took on a throaty rumble.

Tony tried to smile. 'What will you think of next!' He relaxed the pressure of the handkerchief and waited — the nose-bleed had stopped! In a surge of foolhardiness he cried: 'Just look, and I'll show you I really have got hayfever!' To prove it, he sneezed twice, loud and strong — and in horror felt his nose begin to bleed again!

This time, all three vampires had seen it. They all stared with rapt expressions at the dark red blood which flowed from Tony's nose. Just like wild cats waiting to pounce on their prey! thought Tony. He felt himself growing dizzy.

'Has anyone got another handkerchief?' he asked, looking desperately at Anna.

At the sound of his voice, she seemed to wake up from her stupor. In some confusion, she fumbled under her cloak and pulled out a second, smaller cloth. She was going to give it to Tony, but Rudolph snatched it from her hand.

'Have you gone crazy?' he yelled. 'Good red blood?'

'Not a drop must be wasted!' agreed Olga, and with a greedy smile, she came towards Tony.

But Anna moved protectively in front of him.

'I think it's *you* who've gone crazy!' she cried. 'Have you forgotten that Tony's our friend?'

'Friend?' chortled Olga. 'When it comes to blood, friendship stops as far as I'm concerned!' She grabbed Tony by the arm. 'You're not going to begrudge me a little refreshment, even though you'd love to keep it all to yourself, wouldn't you?' she

cried malevolently. 'But you won't stop me
— Tony belongs to me, just to me!'

With that, she pushed Anna aside and,
mouth agape, she advanced on Tony. But
then she stopped in disbelief.

'Where's the blood gone?' she asked.

Tony felt his nose and to his amazement,
it was not bleeding any more. He remembered that once he had read that the best
cure for a nose-bleed is a violent shock. This
saying had certainly proved true for him,
for at the sight of Olga's vampire teeth, his
heart had very nearly stood still. And the
shock of it had made his nose-bleed stop.

'What blood?' he asked cheerfully. 'I told
you I had hayfever!'

With these words, he got up and went to
the bathroom, where he washed away any
revealing traces of blood from his nose.

# 20

# Raise your Glasses!

When he came back to the living room, a
scene of utter shambles met his gaze: all the
cupboard doors were open and the carpet
was strewn with confetti. In the middle of it
all, Olga and Rudolph were bouncing about
on his parents' new sofa as if it were a
trampoline.

'You haven't taken all the glasses out of
the cupboard!' cried Tony.

'Glasses?' giggled Olga. 'Raise your
glasses!' With that, she let off a party
popper in Tony's face. The Little Vampire
let the air slowly out of a red balloon with a
squeak.

'My parents will never let me have a
party again!' wailed Tony.

'Why not?' Olga pretended not to understand.

'They have forbidden me to use the living
room for a party.'

Olga merely tore open another packet of
confetti and sprinkled the contents all over
the sofa.

'Really? I can't understand that. At home
in Transylvania, we always used to hold
our parties in the biggest and nicest room in
the castle.'

'What if my parents came home now?'

'They can join in too!'

'Exactly!' agreed the vampire, giving a particularly high bounce.

'You're so mean!' Tony was near to tears. 'You never think of me!'

'You think so?' smiled Olga. 'Every night I dream of you, of your long white neck. . . .'

'Don't you dream of me?' asked the Little Vampire reproachfully.

'Of you?' she giggled. 'Yes, sometimes.'

Rudolph beamed. 'Do you really?'

'Yes. Whenever I have a nightmare!'

The Little Vampire looked so wounded that in spite of his anger, Tony almost had to laugh at the pair of them.

'And who's going to tidy all this up?' he moaned.

Olga shrugged her shoulders. 'Your mother?' she suggested.

'My mother? You'd be lucky!'

'Then your father and your mother.'

'My parents wouldn't lift a finger.'

'I don't understand why you are so worked up,' she observed, hopping down from the sofa. 'The room looks much cosier now with all these pretty snippets of paper than it did before. I would leave it as it is.'

'You might. But my parents won't. They hate untidiness.'

'Then ask Anna if she'll help you clear up.'

'Anna?' Only now did he realise she was missing. 'Where is she, anyway?'

Olga gave a contemptuous jerk with her head. 'We chucked her out!'

'Chucked her out?' Tony was beside himself. This evening, Anna had been his only ally!

'Because she's a spoilsport.'

'Quite,' agreed the vampire. 'She wouldn't let us have any fun.' And in an attempt at mimicking Anna's voice, he whined: 'Come away from the cupboard! You're not allowed to open the doors! Don't look inside! You're not allowed to take anything out, it doesn't belong to you! Don't climb on the sofa!'

'Yes, so we picked her up and threw her out.'

'You haven't thrown her out of the window?'

'No — just out of the room.'

'So where is she now?'

Olga shrugged her shoulders carelessly. 'She's probably sitting on your bed sulking.'

'On my bed?' It was not a very nice thought. Tony raced off to look.

# 21

# Anna the Spoilsport

When he reached his room, he saw Anna sitting at his desk. Grumpily she lifted her head and said: 'Don't disturb me. I'm reading.'

'Anna, you absolutely must come with me!' he begged.

'I don't have the slightest wish to join in with your party. There are too many people as it is,' she answered coolly.

'No, you must help me!'

'I would much rather read,' she replied pointing to the book. It was *Romeo and Juliet*! 'Do you know it?'

'Me?' Tony was embarrassed. 'Er — I found it rather boring.'

'Yes, the first bit is boring,' she agreed. 'But I whizzed through and found the ending. And that really is something!' Her eyes gleamed. 'Have you read the end?'

'No,' said Tony. He could just imagine why she liked it so much.

'It's a love story,' she explained. 'Romeo and Juliet are in love and will be parted by nothing, not even death.'

'Really?'

'Yes. And when Juliet dies, he follows her to the dark kingdom without the slightest hesitation.'

'But she's only pretending to be dead,' Tony put in.

Anna's expression darkened. 'So you have read it!'

'My father told me the ending.'

She made a gesture of impatience and irritation.

'Pretending or not, they both end up dead. And then they're united forever — just as we two may be one day.'

A cold shudder ran over Tony. 'I thought it was rather a sad ending,' he said hastily.

'Sad?' She looked at him in disbelief. 'It's the loveliest, most heart-warming love story I have ever read!'

'But Romeo and Juliet would much rather have stayed alive. They only had to die because their families were enemies of one another.'

'Pah — alive!' Anna started to cry. 'What's that compared to eternal love?' She got up with a sob and turned her back on Tony. He stood there, helpless. Then he heard a noise in the hallway and all at once, Olga stuck her head round the door.

'Problems?' she asked with a gleeful grin. 'Well, never mind. The most enjoyable part of the evening is about to begin: the Transylvanian Egg and Tomato Dance.' She pointed proudly to a bowl which was full of eggs and tomatoes.

'What are you doing with that? Have you gone completely round the twist?' cried Tony.

Olga laughed happily. 'Yes, we have,' she answered, and disappeared.

'Anna, you've got to help me!' pleaded Tony. Then he ran after Olga.

Back in the living room, she put down the bowl on the table, took out a couple of eggs and tomatoes and jumped onto the sofa.

'Just watch, everybody!' she crowed. 'The Honourable Olga Pigsbubble will now show you the unique, incomparable, Transylvanian. . . .' She got no further, for at that moment, the front doorbell rang.

Olga's smile of self-assurance died. 'Who's that?' she asked suspiciously.

Tony looked perplexed. 'I've no idea. Perhaps it's the neighbours come to complain.'

Now they heard someone banging on the door — someone who sounded very angry. The thumps resounded through the whole flat.

Olga began to tremble like a leaf from top to toe. 'There! They're coming!' she stammered.

'Who?'

'The vampire hunters!' she answered, shaking. She threw the eggs and tomatoes back in the bowl and ran to the window.

'What are you going to do?' cried the Little Vampire.

'Escape!' She tore the window open so violently that two flowerpots came crashing to the floor.

'But we don't have to let them in!' Rudolph put in.

'They'll break down the door!' screeched Olga. She was almost beside herself with fear and had to hold onto the window frame.

'Olga! You can't possibly fly in this state!' the vampire pleaded with her. Once more, the dull thuds could be heard at the front door. Olga gave a shriek and flew away. 'Wait for me, Olga!' called the Little Vampire and flew after her.

Tony was almost pleased, except that the banging on the door came again. Who could it be? Neighbours? The police? He crept fearfully over to the door and called: 'Who's there?'

He heard a giggle. Then a voice said, 'It's me, Anna.'

'Anna?'

'Open up, can't you?' she called, knocking impatiently. Tony opened the door.

'Well, did it work?' she asked with a mischievous grin, and came in.

'What?'

'The trick to get rid of Olga.' She peered into the living room and nodded in satisfaction.

'I haven't the faintest idea what you're talking about,' said Tony.

'Didn't you hear that terrific knocking? It was me!' She laughed and showed Tony her tiny fists. 'It even hurt a bit,' she remarked, 'but for you, I did it gladly.'

'For me?' Tony was perplexed.

'Yes. After all, you did want me to help you.'

'Help me, yes — not go thundering against the door.'

'But that was the trick!' she explained proudly. 'Olga had told us that there was nothing she feared more than the sound of loud knocking against a door.'

'Why?'

'It's something to do with the vampire hunters who burst into her castle and then her parents — well, you know the rest.'

'Poor Olga,' said Tony softly. He had hardly spoken the words, before he went red. To sympathise with Olga was probably the craziest thing he could have done at that moment!

Anna turned on him with blazing eyes. 'Is that all you have to say?' she retorted. 'It doesn't interest you in the slightest that I put my life in danger just to help you!'

'Your life in danger?' stuttered Tony.

'First I had to creep across the hallway without being seen by any of you, and then I had to stand outside for ages hammering on your front door with my fists. Just imagine if someone had caught me out there! They would have thought I was a burglar!'

'It was very nice of you!' said Tony, embarrassed.

'Nice! I hate that word!' she snorted.

'I meant: it was very — ' He hesitated,

99

searching for a flattering expression. 'It was very courageous of you,' he said.

'It was, wasn't it?' She was smiling again.

'I think I ought to start clearing up,' he murmured, moodily surveying the chaos in the living room.

'I'll help you,' Anna offered. 'It'll be quicker with two of us.'

Tony cleared his throat. 'That's really nice — er, lovely of you!'

'Lovely?' repeated Anna with a sigh. 'Oh, Tony. . . .'

# 22

# Tony's Parents

As they crouched together on the carpet picking up the snippets of paper, Tony remarked: 'There's just one thing I'm sorry about.'

'What's that?'

'That now I'll never find out how to do a Transylvanian Egg Dance!'

'Be thankful that you won't!' Anna answered. 'If I know Olga, it would have been beyond a joke!'

'Yes, probably. And having to clear up broken eggs from the carpet would certainly not have been — ' He broke off, for at that moment he heard the front door open.

'My parents!' he exclaimed, turning as white as a sheet. He glanced at the clock: it was only just after ten. 'They never come back this early!' And the living room still looked a complete tip! 'I wish I could vanish into thin air!' he whispered.

'Me too!' agreed Anna with a longing glance at the open window.

They heard the clatter of coat hangers: Tony's parents were still taking off their coats and hanging them in the cupboard.

'Please don't leave me!' begged Tony. 'If you're here, they won't be able to fly off the handle.'

'You think so?' Anna looked doubtful. 'Even when they see my vampire cloak?'

'Oh, they've got used to vampire cloaks by now,' he said.

'Tony?' It was his mother's voice.

'Yes, here,' he answered dolefully.

'Where are you?'

Footsteps hurried towards them — and there stood Tony's parents in the doorway.

'In the living room? But we told you specifically that. . . .' She fell silent and surveyed the scene with wide open eyes. 'This can't be possible! Our beautiful living room. . . .'

'How dare you? What a cheek!' thundered Dad. 'Just look at the carpet! And the flowerpots — broken! As though vandals had ransacked the place. . . .'

Tony tried to make himself as small as possible and looked anxiously at Anna. She had pulled her cloak over her head. Only the tip of her nose could be seen.

'The sofa! It's full of confetti!' shrieked Tony's mother. 'And the cushions look as though someone's bounced all over them!'

Dad gave a cry. 'The record player! I bet they used that too!' He studied Tony with a black expression. 'Am I right?'

Tony wished he could sink into the floor. 'Yes,' he said, trembling.

Suspiciously, his father opened the lid of the record player — and gave another cry. 'It's still going!'

'But — ' began Tony, then stopped. If he said it was all Olga's fault, it would just make matters worse.

'That is the end!' Quite beside himself, Tony's father kept shaking his head. His face had gone red and the corners of his mouth twitched. 'We let you have a party here, we trust you. . . .' Foaming with rage, he towered above Tony. 'And you? Are you out of your mind? Or what is the matter with you?' These last words were said in a bellow. For a second afterwards, everything was quiet.

Then came a gentle little voice. 'Please don't hit him!'

It was Anna. She had drawn her cloak back from her face and faced Tony's father bravely. 'Please don't hit Tony!'

Dad stared at her in bewilderment.

'You?' he said.

'Yes,' replied Anna in a steady voice.

'I've stayed behind especially, to help Tony clear up.'

His parents exchanged glances and before they could say anything, Anna went on: 'It's mean to hit children. Only weaklings do it!'

Tony's father had to smile. 'What makes you think I want to?'

'You looked so fierce.'

'That's true,' agreed Tony's mother. 'When you get cross about something, you can really look quite terrifying.'

'Me? Look terrifying?' Tony's father stroked his chin in some embarrassment. 'Well, in any case, I would never hit Tony.'

'I'm so glad,' sighed Anna. Then she added cheekily: 'Anyway, we were just in the middle of clearing up. If you hadn't come home so early, we would have finished it.'

Tony looked at her sideways in amazement. She did not seem to be at all frightened. On the contrary, it was as if she had overawed his parents by her fearless, self-assured behaviour.

Tony's father was even beginning to look quite cheerful, in spite of the mess. 'Well, we only came back early because we wanted to take a photograph of you all,' he said. 'But where are the other guests?'

'The other guests?' repeated Tony, to play for time. 'Well, er, they — they didn't want to go on. First they made all this mess and then they simply cleared off.'

His mother looked at him disbelievingly. 'Aha — it's always someone else. It never seems to be your fault!'

'No,' he replied truthfully. But of course his mother did not believe him.

'I'm sure you two aren't innocent little angels!' she said.

Anna laughed delightedly. 'No, I certainly am not an angel!'

In the meantime, Tony's father had fetched his camera. 'Stand together over there,' he said, 'so I can take a nice picture of the pair of you . . . Romeo and Juliet!'

'Do you have to?' growled Tony.

'Oh yes!' giggled Anna, standing close up to him.

Dad pressed the button and there was a flash. Anna gave a cry and pressed her hands to her face.

'Ow! My eyes!' she whimpered.

Tony's father lowered the camera in surprise. 'What's up?'

'The light . . . ow, ow, ow, ow!'

'Haven't you ever seen a flash before?'

'A flash?' said Anna, peeping fearfully between her fingers. 'It was so terribly bright — just like the sun.'

'You don't like sun?' remarked Tony's mother.

'No.'

'That's obvious, you're so pale. You ought to go out in the sunshine a bit more often and then you'd get some colour.'

'Me? In the sunshine?' Anna shuddered.

'Yes. Just imagine how awful if would be here on earth without the sun. We would just sit and vegetate in everlasting darkness. Would you like that?'

'I — er, I've got to go,' stammered Anna, walking unsteadily over to the door.

'I'll take you home,' said Dad.

'There's no need,' she answered dully.

'No need? It's almost midnight. You might meet a — vampire!' he added with a wink at Tony.

'I'm not afraid of vampires!' declared Anna.

'I can well believe it,' he said with a laugh. 'They would just think you were one of them — you and your funny cloak. But I will take you home, even if you aren't afraid of vampires.'

He took Anna by the arm. She did not resist. After all, what could she do?

Tony heard the front door close. 'Wait!' he called, following resignedly. 'I'll come with you!'

'Wait a minute! Am I supposed to clear all this up on my own?' called his mother indignantly.

'I'll be right back,' said Tony, and before she could stop him, he had dashed out of the room.

# 23

# Given the Slip!

He ran as fast as he could, but the lift was already on its way down. So he raced down the stairs and arrived at the bottom out of breath. He tore open the door of the building and spied his father walking up and down the footpath, peering in the bushes. Apparently Anna had managed to give him the slip!

'Are you waiting for someone?' Tony asked happily.

'Yes, Anna. She had a stone in her shoe and stopped. I walked on slowly but when I turned back to her, she had vanished.'

Tony had trouble not to laugh. 'She didn't want you to go with her, after all?'

'But it's crazy. A little girl — all alone at this time of night. . . .'

'Anna loves moonlit nights. Whenever it's a full moon, she always goes for a walk.'

His father looked at him sideways in disbelief. 'How old is Anna exactly?'

Tony hesitated. Finally he said: 'About a hundred and fifty.'

'I beg your pardon? Huh, you're just pulling my leg!'

'Well, she might be a hundred and sixty.'

'Okay, okay,' said his father irritably. 'And if I ask you where she lives, you'll tell me, in the cemetery. Is that right?'

'Exactly!' grinned Tony.

'Good,' said Dad craftily, 'then we'll drive to the cemetery straight away.'

Tony gulped. 'What do you want to do?'

'I want to make sure Anna has got home safely.'

'But — '

'Come on. There's the car, over there.'

Tony did not move. 'I think I would rather stay here.'

'Then tell me Anna's address — the right one, mind!'

'Her ad-address?'

'Yes. Do you think I'd let her run off without worrying? Her parents would report me to the police!'

'I'm sure they wouldn't,' said Tony feebly.

'Well, where does she live?'

'Um. . . .' Tony wondered feverishly what he should say. It would be no good giving a false address because his father would simply go up and ring at the door.

'I don't know the name of the street. . . .'

'But you've often been there!'

'Yes — but even so!'

'Then you'll just have to come with me and show me the way.'

Tony tried one last excuse. 'I won't be able to find the way in the dark.'

But his father was not going to give in. 'Rubbish!' he said, striding over to the car. There was nothing left for Tony to do but to follow him.

# 24

# Dark Figures

In the car, his father asked: 'Where to, then?'

Tony wriggled uncomfortably on the back seat. 'Um, well, you go straight up the road first.'

His father started the engine. 'Then where?'

'Th-then left at the traffic lights.'

'But that road does go to the cemetery!'

'Anna lives at the back of — er — behind the cemetery!' He had nearly given it away!

'Are there any residential houses round there?' his father asked doubtfully.

'Of course,' said Tony, although he was not sure himself. But he'd think of something when they got there.

The car slid softly through the night streets. They were deserted and lights still glimmered in only a few houses. This sort of night-time drive could be quite romantic, thought Tony — if only he did not have this strange feeling in his tummy!

All of a sudden, his father laughed. 'Just look over there!'

'Where?'

'Down that little path!'

Now Tony could see two figures standing under a large tree, talking to each other excitedly. They were wearing long black

coats or cloaks, and their faces shimmered palely. Perhaps they were — vampires?

'How funny!' remarked Dad. 'They're wearing the same capes as Anna.'

'Just stop a minute!' cried Tony roughly.

'Why?' asked Dad, but he did drive to the edge of the road.

'Turn off the engine!' implored Tony. His father did so.

At that moment, the two figures turned round and stared over at them.

Tony's father gave a cry. 'But that's Anna!' he said. 'Who's the other one?'

'The — the other one?' stuttered Tony, who was just as surprised as his father. 'That's . . . A-Aunt Dorothy!'

'Anna's aunt?'

'Yes,' said Tony with a shiver. The mere sight of Aunt Dorothy made the cold run down his spine.

His father laughed. 'If it's Anna's aunt, I don't have to worry any more. But even so, I'll just go up and have a quick word with her,' he said, and was about to open the door.

'No!' cried Tony, holding him tightly by the sleeve.

'Why not?'

'Because . . . Anna's aunt is — very shy.'

'So what?' laughed Dad, and got out.

But at once, Aunt Dorothy and Anna turned on their heels and raced off into the darkness. Puzzled, Tony's father stayed near the car. 'Why did they run away from me?' he asked in astonishment.

Tony grinned. 'Perhaps you were making one of your terrifying faces again!'

His father threw him a furious look but said nothing. Undecided, he looked over to the other side of the street. Then he got back into the car. 'Well, I still find that most peculiar,' he remarked. 'But as she's Anna's aunt, I expect she will take Anna home safely.'

'I'm sure she will.'

'Then let's go home.' His father started the car.

'Already?' Tony was enjoying this. 'I was just beginning to have fun.'

His father turned to him with a mischievous grin. 'Clearing up is fun too!'

'Huh!' drawled, Tony. 'Mum will have finished it long ago.'

But unfortunately, he was mistaken. When they went into the living room, his mother was sitting on the sofa with her legs up — and she was reading!

'Did you get Anna home safely?' she asked.

'Yes ... well, no, actually — ' Tony's father faltered. He did not seem to want to admit that Anna had run away from him. 'Anna bumped into her aunt on the way,' he explained finally.

'Her aunt? What a coincidence.'

'Her aunt was very odd. As soon as she saw me, they both ran away. But I'm sure she will have seen Anna home safely.'

'Thank goodness for that!' Tony's mother

gave a sigh of relief. She shut her book with a snap and stood up. Gazing around at all the mess, she remarked: 'I think Tony should go to bed straight away. He's got a lot of clearing up to do tomorrow morning.'

'It's always me!' grumbled Tony, trotting to the door.

'Then ask your friends to come and help you,' suggested his father.

Tony looked at him over his shoulder and said darkly: 'Tomorrow morning? They'll still be in their coffins!'

He heard his mother gasp indignantly.

'Coffins?' laughed his father. 'Is that the latest in beds?'

'Yes,' growled Tony. 'Goodnight.'

# 25

# Cinema

The next day, it rained. Thick cloud hung in the sky and everything was dull and grey — just like Tony's mood. Gloomily he sat at the breakfast table and pushed pieces of toast and honey into his mouth. His mother looked out of the window.

'What a pity!' she said. 'It would happen just when we were going to do something.'

Tony lifted his head with interest. 'Do something with me?'

'You've got to clear up!' she retorted.

'Thanks for reminding me,' said Tony through gritted teeth. 'I had almost forgotten.'

'We could go to the cinema this afternoon,' suggested Dad.

'To the cinema? Oh yes!' exclaimed Tony happily. 'I think there's a vampire film on!'

'A vampire film — that's all I need!' sighed Mum.

Tony's father laughed. 'What do you mean? That could be just the right entertainment for a rainy Sunday.'

Guardedly, Tony's mother asked: 'What sort of film is it? It's bound to be some hopeless thing with tons of tomato ketchup sprayed about.'

'But that's what makes it fun!' giggled Tony.

'And what's more, you'll be able to have endless discussions about it afterwards, if it's been on Tony's favourite subject,' put in Dad.

She hesitated. 'I don't know.' Then after a pause, she said, 'Perhaps you're right. Perhaps I really should see one of these films so I can find out what's asked of kids in these films nowadays.'

'Oh great!' Tony was over the moon.

'But first you've got to tidy up,' she said, 'so that we can get into our living room again.'

'Tidy up? No problem!' he answered cheerfully and got down from the table.

'One night a great big vampire boy came dancing up to me!' he sang as he set to work. He was very pleased: an amusing afternoon was in store and he would not even have to pay for his ticket.

When they came out of the cinema at six o'clock, Tony began to doubt that it had been such a good idea after all. His mother's face was ashen. Once in the car, she turned the conversation immediately to Anna and Rudolph. 'Your funny friends now seem even more mysterious,' she said.

'What do you mean?' Tony pretended not to understand.

'Their cloaks, their pale faces — everything about them looks exactly as it did in that film.'

He tried to laugh. 'Anna and Rudolph like going to the cinema too!'

'I've never once met them in daylight,' she went on thoughtfully. 'And then there's that strange smell that comes off them. . . .'

'Oh, that's just children's fun and games,' replied Dad. 'The pair of them enjoy making themselves look different.'

'Exactly!' agreed Tony in relief. 'At school the teachers are always saying that you shouldn't be prejudiced against people who look different.'

His mother looked at him in some annoyance but said nothing. She started the engine and drove carefully out of their parking place. It was still raining, so she switched on the windscreen wipers.

'Oh dear, those poor vampires!' teased Dad. 'Their cloaks must get wet through in this weather. I bet they'll have to go round on foot tonight.'

'Very funny!' snapped Tony's mother crossly. But suddenly she had to put on her brakes sharply: a figure in a long dark cape had hurried across the street in front of the car.

'Did you see that?' grinned Dad. 'That was the first vampire!'

She turned her head towards him and said softly and carefully: 'Oh, do you think so? Then you obviously weren't paying attention during the film.'

'Why?'

'Because the sun hasn't gone down yet!'

# 26

# Raindrops Tapping on the Window

It was still raining when Tony was lying in his bed. His eyes wide open, he listened in the darkness. The drops tapped steadily against the window, lulling him to sleep. But then the tapping became so loud and insistent that he sat up crossly. 'How can anyone go to sleep with that racket?' he growled. Then it occurred to him that it might not be the rain that was knocking on his window. . . .

He leapt out of bed and pulled the curtain aside — and it was true. There on the window-sill sat Anna. Her face was glistening wet but she was smiling. Tony opened the window. Now he could see that she was wearing a large black macintosh cloak, and she had pulled the hood over her head.

'Hello, Tony,' she said gently.

'You?' he murmured. 'I thought vampires couldn't fly in the rain. . . .'

'Why ever not?' she replied. 'We just have to put on our waterproofs. Here, I've brought one for you,' she added, holding out a second macintosh cloak.

'For me?' he asked, startled.

'Yes. Tonight you've got to help me.'

'Me? But — ' He looked over at the door. Back in the living room, his parents were sitting in front of the television.

118

'Last night Olga suddenly took to her heels,' she told him in a whisper. 'And now Rudolph is wandering about the cemetery in complete despair, and won't eat till Olga comes back.'

'But that could be really dangerous!' exclaimed Tony.

'And he hasn't even put his waterproofs on! If McRookery and Sniveller find him now, he won't be able to fly away, because his cloak is soaked through.'

Tony was silent, in a daze. 'What about your parents? Don't they look after you?' he asked finally.

She shook her head. 'You know what it's like with us. Everyone has enough to do, looking after themselves. That's why you've got to talk to him!'

Tony hesitated. 'Has Olga really gone for good?'

'Yes, luckily.'

'Because of yesterday, when you hammered on the door?'

'Yes,' said Anna, adding impatiently, 'now will you come, before something happens to Rudolph?'

'Wait!' Tony went to the door and turned the key. Then he put on his jumper, trousers and trainers.

'What's taking you so long?' asked Anna nervously.

'Nothing,' he answered quickly and came to the window. She handed him a vampire cloak. 'That's Uncle Theodore's cloak, the one Olga had. And you put the waterproof one on top.'

Deftly she put the two cloaks on him. The waterproof one was extraordinarily light, Tony could hardly feel it. Cautiously he made a couple of arm movements and found he was floating.

'So you really can fly in these!' he said doubtfully.

Anna laughed softly. 'But of course. We've used these waterproofs for a hundred years and no one has fallen down yet!'

Tony did not find this information particularly comforting. 'It's so cramped under here,' he complained.

'You'll get used to it,' she replied.

Tony looked out at the streaming rain and sighed. In this sort of weather, you would not even turn a dog away from the door! He threw a last longing look at his warm dry bed — and then away they flew.

# 27

# A Secret Signature

The rain seemed to be coming from all directions. Tony tried to fly calmly and steadily, but the huge heavy drops struck him right in the face.

'Blow it, I can't see a blooming thing!' he muttered through clenched teeth, and wiped his eyes with his hand.

'Fly right behind me!' called Anna.

'My arm — I've got caught up in the cloak!'

'Wait, I'll help you.' She flew to his side. 'Give me your hand.'

Trembling, he stretched his hand out. She gripped it and pulled him along with her. Tony's heart was thudding in his chest. He had so nearly gone tumbling down to the ground. ...

'We're almost there,' he heard Anna say. As if through a thick veil, he saw the old wall of the cemetery below them. They flew down over it and landed in the far side of the cemetery.

'Was it bad?' Anna asked sympathetically.

Tony freed his hand from hers. 'No,' he lied. There was no need for her to know that he had just been scared to death!

'I think flying in the rain is very exciting,' she declared. 'But right now we must find Rudolph.' She went on ahead, and Tony followed with trembling knees.

Suddenly Anna stopped.

'My headstone — someone has put it upright!'

Tony had to grin. 'Really?'

'Yes. And all the moss has been scraped off it.'

She walked round the stone in amazement. Then she bent down and picked up the clay figure with a cry of surprise.

'But it's a vampire!' she exclaimed. 'Do you know how it got here?'

Tony merely grinned.

'There's something inside it!' she said excitedly. She pulled out the piece of paper and began to read: 'Dear Anna, I must talk to you. I'm sorry about Olga, really I am. Tony.'

With eyes wide in amazement, she looked at him. 'Is the letter from you?'

'Me?' Tony was most uncomfortable. She would have to read the letter now!

'Why do you think that?'

'Because your name's on it.'

'My name?'

'Yes, here,' she said, holding out the piece of paper.

'I can't see anything,' he replied, stifling a smile. For in the meantime the rain had made the ink run, so that the signature was now totally illegible — thank goodness!

Anna stared at the piece of paper in disbelief. 'But it was there just now. . . .'

Tony shrugged his shoulders gleefully. 'Perhaps it was a secret signature,' he said,

adding cryptically, 'anyway, it's much too dark to read. You'll only ruin your eyesight.'

Anna folded the letter with a knowing smile and stuck it back in the clay figure. Then she hid it carefully under her cloak. 'Thank you,' she said, and gazed at him so tenderly that he felt quite peculiar.

"Sall right,' he muttered in embarrassment. 'Oughtn't we to look for Rudolph?'

'Yes. Come on.'

# The Pangs of Love

She set off in determination and Tony had trouble following her. It was true, the rain had slackened, but the ground was so soft that several times his trainers were stuck fast. He was amazed at how lightly Anna was able to run on ahead of him. The muddy ground did not seem to make the slightest difference to her. He wondered if it had anything to do with the old-fashioned shoes she was wearing.

'Not so fast!' he called, then stumbled and fell — right smack into a puddle!

When he had scrambled to his feet once more, his hands and trousers were covered in mud.

'Have you hurt yourself?' Anna asked in concern.

'No,' he growled. 'I've just had a bath, that's all.'

She giggled. 'Wasn't the rain enough for you?'

'It's all in aid of camouflage,' he declared with as much dignity as he could muster. 'So that no one will be able to see my hands in the dark.'

Anna studied his hands, laughed and set off again. With gritted teeth, Tony slid after her. By then he was so wet that he did not care any more.

At the chapel, Anna turned off to the left, into the new part of the cemetery which Tony never usually visited. Here the paths were as dead-straight as if they had been drawn with a ruler, and each grave looked like the window of a flower shop.

'Do you really think Rudolph is round here?' he whispered.

'See that weeping willow?' she answered, equally quietly.

He nodded.

'Under it there's a bench,' she went on. 'He sometimes goes and sits there when he's got a problem.'

'Does he often have — problems, then?' asked Tony in surprise.

'Of course, like all normal vampires,' she replied. 'But usually it's only a row with our parents or Greg. Nothing really bad. But this time, with Olga. . . .'

She said no more. Tony shivered. 'I just hope we're not too late,' he whispered and the thought of it made him swallow hard.

Anna did not reply. She was standing still, listening.

'Can you hear anything?' asked Tony in a quavery voice.

'I don't know. Perhaps it's just the rain . . . but it sounds as though someone's crying.'

Tony listened as well, but he could only hear the patter of the rain.

'I'll just go and look,' she said. 'You wait here.'

And before Tony could say anything, she disappeared.

He went and stood behind a hedge, and waited. The minutes seemed to go on forever. At last he heard Anna's voice. 'Tony, where are you?'

'Here,' he said, coming out of his hiding place.

'It is Rudolph,' she said in a whisper.

A weight fell from Tony's mind. 'Well? Did you speak to him?'

'No. You must go and talk to him. Come on, I'll take you.'

She gave him a smile of encouragement. Then she went on ahead of Tony who took great care not to give himself away by any noise. So they finally reached the willow tree and Tony saw the Little Vampire. He was sitting on the bench like a little heap of misery, his head buried in his hands, sobbing.

It was such a wretched sight that Tony looked to Anna for help. But the place where she had been standing just a moment before was empty. At first he was startled, then he felt rather relieved: it would certainly be more simple to talk to Rudolph without Anna standing right next to them.

He took a step forward and said: 'Rudolph? It's me, Tony.'

The Little Vampire lifted his head and looked at Tony out of small, swollen eyes. His face was awash with tears — or were they drops of rain? 'What do you want?' he asked in a tired voice.

'I . . . ' began Tony, and stopped. How on earth did you comfort a lovesick vampire? 'I wanted — well, I just wanted to tell you we two are friends. And friendship means you stick by one another.'

'I haven't any friends any more,' replied the vampire, and the corners of his mouth began to twitch. 'I'm alone in the world, utterly alone.' And with a sob, he hid his face in his hands.

'But of course you've got friends!' said Tony. 'You've got me — and Anna. And that's worth a heap more than some stuck-up girl from Transylvania, who runs off at the first opportunity and leaves you in the lurch!'

'Stuck up?' cried the Little Vampire. 'Left me in the lurch?' With tears in his eyes, he blazed at Tony: 'You just want to do Olga down!'

'Me? I certainly don't!' Tony reassured him. Secretly he was pleased that he had managed to rouse the Little Vampire from his gloom and despair. A blustering, abusive Rudolph was heaps better than a fed-up and depressed one!

'So you two claim to be my friends?' the Little Vampire now exclaimed, jumping up from the bench in a rage. 'You and Anna — it's your fault that Olga's flown away!'

'So? Be grateful for small mercies!' retorted Tony, somewhat foolishly as he soon realised.

The Little Vampire gave a bloodcurdling

yell. He grabbed Tony by the shoulders and shook him. 'You — you — ' he snorted. 'If you ever say that again, I'll — '

'Ow, you're hurting me!' cried Tony, trying to free himself from the vampire's grip. But it was no use: the vampire's fingers were clamped to him like a vice.

'If you ever say anything foul about Olga again, I'll just blow your life out like a candle,' he said, and blew a puff of deathly breath right in Tony's face.

It made Tony cough. 'Anyway, Olga wanted to leave you!' he croaked.

'Leave me? How do you know?'

'Because she told me.'

Startled, the vampire let his arms sink to his sides. 'When?'

Tony took a deep breath before answering. 'When she was over with me.'

'Yes, well?' cried the vampire huskily, cracking his bony fingers in a frenzy.

Tony tried hard to keep a serious face. Of course Olga had not told him anything of the sort, but perhaps this way he could help Rudolph get over the pangs of love more quickly.

'She told me she was going to visit a cousin — in Paris.'

'A cousin? In Paris?' repeated the vampire. 'What was his name?' he asked suspiciously.

'She didn't tell me,' answered Tony.

'She never said anything to me about a cousin,' murmured the Little Vampire. 'Nor about Paris.... After all, do they even have cemeteries there?' he said, turning enquiringly to Tony.

'Of course they do,' he answered, adding playfully, 'even ones with double beds... er, graves!'

'Hmmm,' said the vampire thoughtfully. 'That would explain Olga's reserve towards me... I had already suspected there might be another vampire in her life....'

'That's right,' confirmed Tony. 'Right from the start Olga wanted to join this cousin, but the journey to Paris was a bit too far for her. That's why she arranged a stopover with you.'

Rudolph's eyes filled with tears once more.

'A stopover,' he said in a choking voice. 'And I thought — ' He stopped and pulled a handkerchief out from under his cloak. 'Thank you for telling me all this,' he said, blowing his nose. 'Now I really do know that you are my friend.'

He sighed deeply, then slowly, almost as if in his sleep, he walked away. Before he was swallowed up in the darkness, he turned round one last time. 'See you, Tony,' he said.

'Yeah, see you,' replied Tony.

Then Tony heard a rustling and suddenly Anna was standing beside him.

'That cousin in Paris was a brilliant idea of yours!' she said.

Tony went red. 'Did you hear everything?'

'Almost everything,' she answered, 'you were talking so loudly. But I didn't want to eavesdrop — I only stayed nearby to make sure no one disturbed you.'

'I want to go home,' said Tony. His teeth were chattering and he suddenly felt very cold.

Anna looked at him tenderly. 'I'll come with you,' she said.